Ghosts, premonitions and things that go bump in the night are guaranteed to put a shiver down your spine as you meet . . . Tamsin, whose new friend gives her a friendship necklace with a difference; Ben, who is haunted by the face of a friend in trouble; Tommy and Titch, who set out to walk in the Wild Place and face the fearsome Wodwo; and many other surprising characters and events.

This brilliant collection of short stories comes from a haunted house full of top authors, including Malorie Blackman, Brian Morse, Paul Stewart, Jan Mark and Helen Dunmore.

Also available from Tony Bradman,
and published by Corgi Books:

FANTASTIC SPACE STORIES

GRIPPING WAR STORIES

PHENOMENAL FUTURE STORIES

SENSATIONAL CYBER STORIES

FOOTBALL FEVER

FOOTBALL FEVER 2

FOOTBALL FEVER 3

GOOD SPORTS! A BAG OF SPORTS
STORIES

INCREDIBLY CREEPY STORIES

**COLLECTED BY
TONY BRADMAN**

Illustrated by Peter Dennis

CORGI BOOKS

INCREDIBLY CREEPY STORIES
A CORGI BOOK : 0 552 54964 9

First published in Great Britain by Doubleday,
a division of Transworld Publishers

PRINTING HISTORY
Doubleday edition published 1996
Corgi edition published 1997

This edition Produced for the Book People Ltd,
Hall Wood Avenue, Haydock, St Helens WA11 9UL

Corgi Books are published by Random House Children's Books,
61–63 Uxbridge Road, Ealing, London W5 5SA,
a division of The Random House Group Ltd,
in Australia by Random House Australia (Pty) Ltd,
20 Alfred Street, Milsons Point, Sydney, NSW 2061, Australia,
in New Zealand by Random House New Zealand Ltd,
18 Poland Road, Glenfield, Auckland 10, New Zealand
and in South Africa by Random House (Pty) Ltd,
Endulini, 5a Jubilee Road, Parktown 2193, South Africa.

Made and printed in Great Britain by
Cox & Wyman Ltd, Reading, Berkshire.

CONTENTS

EMILY BITES
by Stephen Bowkett

'She looks rosy she looks rosy, she looks happy she
looks happy, she looks dreamy she looks dreamy,
she looks pale she looks pale . . .'

I could hear the voices chanting right from the end
of the street. They were getting higher as the song
went on. It was an old song, without much of a tune,
and I'd heard it plenty of times before. It came from
an age when the people lived in superstition and fear.
It was a song that was supposed to be able to banish
vampires from the town . . .

'She looks weary she looks weary, she looks dying
she looks dying, she looks dead she looks dead . . .'

Even though I thought the song was a load of
old rubbish, I hurried along the street to find out
what was going on. Kids usually chanted it in

7

the playground, along with Ring-O-Roses, Tom Thumbkins, Little Shona Morgan and all kinds of others.

I swung round the corner of Maple Street and saw about ten children gathered around someone whose face I couldn't see. I recognized most of the kids: some of them were in the same year as me at Smallwood High. And there was Harry Henderson who was twelve, and so two years older than I was, with his little brother Billy and younger sister Susie. They all formed a kind of gang, and over the past couple of months had let me hang around with them. At first I'd felt uneasy, being a new kid, and because of some of the things Henderson had said. I'd come to believe the local people were really suspicious of strangers – frightened, even. But I'd played it cool and showed I was friendly. Gradually they'd come to accept me. Being among these kids felt comfortable now, felt good . . . Or had done, until I'd turned the corner.

I reckoned that Henderson should have known better, teaching the younger ones pointless, cruel songs like that.

I walked up to the group and stood where I could see what was going on. Tony Holmes glanced round at me as I arrived and he grinned. I didn't smile back, but stared past him at the girl who was crouched in the middle of the circle, her hands over her face, and her long dark hair falling across her fingers.

'She looks smiling she looks smiling, she looks risen she looks risen, she looks flying she looks flying, she looks gone she looks gone—'

'Why don't you cut it out?' I said. I was feeling annoyed and kind of embarrassed that some of my friends should behave like this. And I felt sorry for the girl, whoever she was, because when I'd moved into Smallwood six months ago I had suffered the same treatment.

'Never to return – never to return – never to return—'

'Stop it!' I yelled, forcing my way into the ring, standing between the crouching girl and Harry Henderson, who I guessed had started it all.

'Never to return,' Henderson said, 'never to return . . . Stay out of it, Beech. This is none of your business.'

'Of course it is! I'm one of you – I'm in the gang. And anyway, behaving like this can give the entire town a bad name.'

'Clear off, Beech,' Tony Holmes told me. I stayed firmly where I was.

'How would you like to be bullied?' I challenged them. 'Why can't you leave her alone, she's done nothing to you!'

'*Her* kind,' Henderson said with a sneer, 'hurt *our* kind. They always have, and they always will. Ask anyone.'

'What are you talking about?' I asked sharply.

'Just because she's a stranger doesn't mean she's a danger . . .' I smiled self-consciously as I said that. It was a little rhyme that Mr Brandner, my teacher, had taught the class when I'd arrived. He made them all chant it: 'Just because he's a stranger doesn't mean he's a danger.' It sounded odd saying it for someone else's benefit.

'She's not the same as we are,' Susie Henderson piped up in her squeaky little voice. 'Harry says so.'

'Harry's talking out of his left ear,' I snapped at her. 'You're old enough to know better, Susie. And as for—'

Henderson pushed the flat of his hand into my chest, making me stagger back. I bumped into the girl and fell back, hitting my head against one of the trees in the avenue.

That did it. Henderson was bigger than me, and probably stronger, but suddenly I wasn't scared of him – I was furious with him for his mean jokes and cruel taunts, just like I'd been when he and his pals had once chanted the vampire song in a ring around me.

He didn't expect me to come back at him, and was taken by surprise. I saw his hands fly up to protect his face as I smacked my fist bang into his nose.

Henderson howled, but all the other kids laughed and cheered, and I think that's what saved me. Rather than make a fight of it, Henderson stared in shock at the blood dripping down onto his shirt. He wiped

10

furiously at his nose and tried to flick the blood away, as his big bully's eyes swam with tears and his lip began to tremble.

'Harry is a cissy, Harry is a cissy!' Angela Stevens started the tease going and everyone took it up. Henderson glared at them, then made an expression of pain and looked sorry for himself as he hurried off – turning back once to jab a bloody finger at me.

'I'm telling my dad on you, Beech! And I'm gonna get you for this!'

'You deserved it, Harry,' I told him quietly.

'We protect our own,' he replied, then yelled at me: 'And if you think you're one of us after this – you can whistle!'

We all watched him go. Some of the kids followed him in straggly ones and twos. 'Go home,' I said to the others. 'Go and play your stupid games somewhere else.'

They didn't argue. Not because they thought I'd hit them, but because – I hoped – they felt ashamed.

As they wandered away, I helped the girl to her feet.

She was a little older than me, and taller. Rather thin. And she looked very pale, probably since her hair was so black, but also because Henderson and his crew must have really frightened her badly. The red zip-up jacket she wore was dusty, and there was a tear in her jeans at the knee.

'I'm – sorry,' I said with a shrug.

'Why should you be sorry?' Her voice was calm and soft, the words rounded with an unusual accent I couldn't quite place. I thought to myself that she wasn't really a pretty girl, but she was striking: pale and tall and quiet . . . And a stranger, which it seemed was the worst thing to be in the nowhere town of Smallwood.

'I'm sorry this is the welcome you got. Some people just don't think at all.'

She shrugged also, and pushed her hair back out of her eyes.

'What's your name?' she asked.

'Beech. Everyone calls me that.'

'But what's your first name?'

I stared at my trainers. 'Um, you wouldn't want to know . . . I don't like my first name much.'

'OK, Beech,' she chuckled. 'I'm Emily. Pleased to meet you. Thanks for saving me.'

'No problem . . . So what's your last name, Emily?'

'You wouldn't want to know,' she said, and we both laughed.

She reached her hand out and I thought for a second she wanted me to shake it. But her hand lifted up and up and a cool finger touched my lower lip, wiping off a spot of Henderson's blood.

Emily looked at the blood spot with wide brown eyes. Standing there on the empty street on that autumn afternoon, I felt a shiver hurry through me. I wondered, just for an instant, if what Harry had said – and if the chant – might be true after all. But that was really stupid. Maybe some of Henderson's small-mindedness had rubbed off on me, was the answer.

Then Emily wiped her finger on her jeans, and cocked her head a little sideways.

'I'll see you around then, Beech. Maybe you can give me a tour of the town some time?'

'Glad to,' I said, wondering if making a friend of her really would ruin my chances with the gang. 'Anyway, I've got to go now. Bye.'

I turned and began walking towards home. Then it occurred to me that I had no idea where Emily lived. So I stopped and looked round to shout after her.

But she'd gone.

Mum and Dad and I had moved out here to get away from the smoke and the noise of the big city. Dad had worked as an accountant for a large firm and Mum did supply teaching in local schools. But they'd both wanted something else – not just a quiet life, or even an easy life; but clean air, good friends, nice views out of the window, and a sense of belonging.

Smallwood seemed to provide all of that. We passed through it once on a touring holiday and liked what we saw. We'd sold up shortly afterwards and bought a house on Maple Street. Soon after, my parents had opened a grocery store in the shopping centre. It took me a long time to get used to seeing Dad in casual slacks and shirt rather than a blue pinstripe suit! But both of them loved it, being part of the life of the town. Maybe adults are different. Maybe they don't let crazy ideas rule their lives: crazy ideas and mindless superstitions.

I helped out in the shop during school holidays, and because Smallwood was not overrun with cars, Mum let me deliver grocery orders on my bike. Dad fitted a basket at the front and panniers at the sides, but I could take all these off if I wanted to . . . Panniers and a front basket are definitely uncool when you're cruising!

I did some deliveries that afternoon and got back to the shop just before it closed. Dad was in the stock room unpacking boxes. Mum, behind the counter, looked tired out.

'What a day! Your father and I have been rushed off our feet and the place has been packed. It must be the anniversary, I suppose . . .'

I opened my mouth to ask what anniversary, but then I remembered the project we'd been doing at school that half-term. Smallwood was founded four hundred years ago as nothing more than a couple of shacks in a clearing in the forest. The early settlers, so the local history books said, struggled hard to carve out an existence for themselves; felling trees, planting some crops, farming pigs and chickens and sheep. Mr Brandner told us stories of those times. He said that it wasn't just the harshness of the conditions that made life difficult. The forest was full of wolves then – and other predators, Mr Brandner said – before they'd been hunted to extinction. The settlers had fought desperately on many occasions to drive away the wolf packs that roamed the land in search of food.

I put my hand up and pointed out that there was not a single recorded instance of a wolf killing a person. I'd read that in a book about conservation.

Mr Brandner smiled his wide, white-toothed smile at me, and cocked his head a little sideways.

'Well, there are plenty of accounts in the museum archives of Smallwood settlers being set upon by ferocious animals. Maybe bears in some cases, but as for all the other occasions – if not wolves, then what else?'

I had no answer to that. Mr Brandner went on to explain that in later times, bands of robbers and highwaymen had plagued Smallwood when it had grown from a settlement into a town . . .

No wonder the people were still suspicious of strangers, I thought, and liked to keep themselves to themselves. Then I shook my head. That was centuries ago. There was no danger from newcomers now – or wolves, or whatever the predators had been . . . was there?

Emily called in at the shop next day, which was a Friday. The anniversary celebrations were set to start that evening and last all through the weekend. My parents, like other shopkeepers, were decorating their shelves and stringing up bunting across the road outside.

'Hi,' I said. 'What can I get you?'

'I was hoping you might show me round the town later, this evening maybe, if you have time . . .'

'Um.' I hesitated. I'd been intending to bike round, find the gang, and try to make things up with them. Having to trail about with Emily could be kind of embarrassing.

'If I'm going to be accepted here, I need to know the place, don't I?' she argued reasonably, then smiled and stared around the shop.

'I mean, you have some really *weird* local customs.'

'Such as?' I almost felt offended, to be told Mum's decorations looked weird.

Emily shrugged lightly. 'Oh, like all the blue strips of tissue paper you've hung up. It's the same in every shop. And there, those ropes of garlic . . .'

Mum came through from the stock room in time to hear what Emily was saying.

'I'm told,' Mum said, 'that the blue paper represents running water. It crops up in folklore all over the world. Apparently wolves and wildcats and other creatures are frightened to swim across it. Many early settlers must have risked their lives – and saved their lives – by swimming a fast-flowing stream to escape wild animals. As for the garlic – it does wonders for a pizza or a stew!'

Mum laughed, and I sort of giggled awkwardly. Emily stared curiously at the paper strips. Then the bell tinkled and the front door opened. It was Mrs Holmes, with Tony at her side, laden with shopping. Tony saw me talking with Emily and his familiar grin appeared. I blushed, but then thought – why should I feel conspicuous just because Emily's a girl?

I said, loudly so that Tony could hear, 'Yeah, I'll show you round. Tonight, at six, before it gets too dark . . .'

Mrs Holmes' eyebrows lifted as she glanced at my mother, then she shook her head slightly, as though it was a signal, and her large gold earrings glinted in the light.

Emily's eyes sparkled with pleasure at my offer, but over her shoulder I could see Tony looking daggers at me. He put down his mother's bag of shopping and made the sign of the cross in the air.

Actually, I felt pretty safe going out that evening. As soon as the shops closed up and folks got home from work, the street parties began. Paper lanterns glowed in every front garden, and lots of families were letting off fireworks. Scores of people were out on the pavements, passing by our house, some of them carrying scarecrow-like figures on poles, made from straw and cardboard and old clothes.

'What do they represent?' I asked Mum, but she was as much in the dark as I was.

17

'Never bothered to ask . . . What big teeth they have,' she said, pointing through the lounge window at the face on one of them, drawn with a kid's crayons.

Along the road, cars were moving at a crawl, headlights blazing, horns blaring.

The town's strange customs unnerved me, I realized, because I didn't understand them. I found it odd that Mr Brandner had told the class nothing about these traditions. But I guessed it was too late now for me to duck out of showing Emily the sights . . .

I'd explained to Mum and Dad what had happened yesterday on the corner. They thought it was a good idea for me to take Emily around the town, 'So that she won't think *all* the people here are wary of newcomers.'

'But don't be out long,' Dad said, and I nodded.

I went into the hall to fetch my jacket. The phone rang as I was passing.

'Hello, 7724—'

'She looks dreamy she looks dreamy, she looks pale she looks pale, she looks weary she looks weary, she looks dead she looks—'

'Who is this?'

'Watch you don't get bitten, Beech. Just remember that. Watch you don't get bitten!'

I slammed the receiver down and snatched my jacket off the hook. I'd recognized Henderson's

18

voice, and realized Tony must have told him of my plans.

I'd arranged to meet Emily outside our shop, which was just a couple of minutes' walk away from the house. The shopping centre was quieter than the surrounding streets: the shadows were darker in doorways and side alleys; the sounds of celebration grew muffled and distant.

As I walked into the empty mall, I felt myself tensing up. Above me, strung across from shop to shop, the anniversary bunting was fluttering in the breeze. The sound reminded me of bats' wings, or the soft flapping of a vampire's cloak.

I laughed at my own fear and thought how stupid I was being, letting Henderson get to me like this. Who'd want to be part of a sad gang like his anyway! . . . I walked firmly towards the shop doorway . . .

. . . And a figure suddenly stepped out in front of me, sending a bolt of panic right through me like lightning.

'Oh, sorry,' Emily said, 'did I frighten you?'

'No, just startled me. I wasn't expecting you to be waiting here alone, in the dark.'

'The night doesn't scare me, Beech. It never has.'

She was dressed up in a long black coat, and her hair was tucked down behind the collar out of sight. I caught myself thinking that she looked almost pretty . . .

'I can't be out too long,' I said.

19

'Me neither.'

'And we ought to get in among the crowds. You never know who's lurking around – even though the people here are friendly,' I added quickly.

'Friendly?' Emily smiled a wide and disbelieving smile. I noticed how white her teeth were . . . And was she wearing a touch of lipstick, or were her lips really that red?

'Yes, yes, they are friendly, when you get to know them.'

'And how well do *you* know them?' she wondered out loud.

I swallowed hard. 'Um, come on. I'll show you the sights. Don't worry, everyone's having a good time. You'll soon see what they're really like.'

I strode across the shopping centre with Emily by my side, regretting my promise to her now. We reached the main street and wandered with the masses of townspeople towards the middle of Smallwood. There they all gathered in the Memorial Square, around the ornamental flower beds and the stone slab that had been laid there in remembrance and respect of the founding fathers of the town.

I showed Emily the slab close up. Into the granite were carved the words: 'To Those Whose Lives Were Lost So We Might Survive'.

Then a kind of stillness settled over the people and the atmosphere changed. It felt colder suddenly. Or maybe it was just me . . .

'Come on,' I whispered, 'this isn't for us.'

I led Emily away along Market Street, where I was able to point out the old town hall and the site of the cattle market, and the very imposing-looking museum. Not far away was the school. We walked over there and peered at the big redbrick Victorian building through the locked iron gates.

'I suppose you'll be starting there next week?' She nodded but didn't reply. 'Will you have far to come?'

'We live out on Endore Street, last house on the left. It isn't too far.'

I was feeling uneasy again, because something was different, though I couldn't pinpoint quite what it was. Perhaps Henderson's words were coming back to haunt me . . . Watch you don't get bitten, Beech. *Watch you don't get bitten* . . .

'Well,' I said, pointing into the gloom, 'the building's not much, but there's a brilliant playing-field. It goes right down to the river, and there are woods beyond . . .'

I looked at Emily and realized she was a mystery to me: I knew I had to find out about her, one way or the other.

'Emily . . .'

Her eyes were glittering in the streetlight. They were very intense, burning into me.

'Emily . . . You wanted to know my first name . . . It's Leonard. OK, I've said it . . . Now you know why I prefer Beech!'

I grinned foolishly, as a terrible tightness gripped my insides. 'Tell me,' I said faintly, 'tell me your secret . . .'

Emily moved a little closer, and all the sound seemed to drain out of the air. I was trembling as I thought, she's going to do it – she's going to bite me now!

Her mouth moved towards my neck, my ear.

The whole universe became very cold and still.

'It's Hononletter,' she whispered.

I stepped back. 'What?'

'My last name, it's Hononletter.'

I stood there for a moment, stunned. Then the awful squeezing feeling inside me burst like a balloon and I laughed helplessly, doubling over, the tears streaming down my face.

Emily was laughing too, just as much – but then her face twisted into an expression of horror. And she screamed.

I whirled around and saw a gang of kids running towards us. They were coming fast, much too fast, and there was something very odd about them. Terrifyingly odd.

'It's Tony Holmes,' I told Emily, 'and Barry Longhurst – Angela Stephens – the little Hendersons . . . But . . . But—'

The running children began to growl as soon as we saw them. Susie Henderson started barking. Her brother Billy howled at us, but the howling was quickly changing, growing deeper and fiercer – as Billy's face changed to match it, his eyes turning red, his mouth pushing out into a black muzzle with terrible, powerful jaws.

I heard someone yelling above the noise, and realized it was me. Emily grabbed my hand as she attempted to drag me away.

'Let's try to reach the main street—' she started to say, before we both froze in disbelief.

What seemed to be the entire population of Smallwood was streaming towards us; a great dark mass of bodies melting into new shapes, sprouting wiry fur, red and black and silvery white. Dozens of eyes – hundreds of eyes – glowed like embers in the dark. And white teeth flashed, and red tongues lolled hungrily.

The wind gusted, bringing the heat of the pack in a stifling wave across our faces; bringing the sharp smell of the beasts to our nostrils.

'There's a side gate—' I realized as I said it. 'Maybe we can outrun them – find somewhere to hide!' It was a desperate hope, I knew, but our only hope.

I had a wild idea we'd be safe by midnight, because perhaps the people of Smallwood transformed to show their true selves only once in a generation, or once in a hundred years. It made sense. Just as human beings had wiped out ordinary wolves, so they would surely destroy werewolves – man-wolves – if the secret escaped. And for centuries the pack had

been clever, keeping itself to itself, going about the ordinary business of an ordinary town: making strangers feel unwelcome, so that those strangers would go away and leave them in peace . . .

I took Emily's hand and for a few metres we dashed *towards* the pack, until we came to the side gate I knew was always left unlocked.

I kicked it open and started running towards the building, hoping Emily didn't slow us down . . . I was amazed to find that she not only kept pace with me, but could easily outrun me, so that it felt as though I was almost gliding along the ground, my feet hardly touching.

Within a few minutes we had left the pack far behind, and paused for a moment in the shadow of the school building.

'Rest – just for a – while,' I gasped. 'Then we – can—'

The shadows moved beside us and a hunched shape stepped out. Its mouth opened wide and I smelled its hot meaty breath.

'I warned you not to get bitten, Beech,' Henderson growled, human words twisted by his animal's mouth.

I shrieked in total panic. Henderson's jaws opened further and he smiled. It was a smile that was big enough to swallow my head.

I thought that was it: Emily and I were done for. The pack was closing in – and there was Mrs Holmes running at the head of it. Her black muzzle was drawn back in fury, and her gold earrings still twinkled on her pointed, fur-covered ears.

Something happened then, so quickly I hardly saw it.

Henderson lunged towards us: there was teeth and fur and flashing eyes.

I flinched away as Emily lashed out. And amazingly, Henderson staggered back, howling in his pain.

'Beech, come with me!'

Emily took my hand once more, and I didn't argue. We raced on, away from the school towards the park. The lights of the town dwindled behind us. The sound of the wind in the woods and the busy splashing of the stream grew louder up ahead.

'The bridge,' Emily said urgently. '*Where's the bridge?*'

'There isn't a bridge!' I yelled at her.

She stopped, not even out of breath, and stared at me.

'You have to go five miles along the River Road to cross,' I explained. 'But why does that . . . matter?'

I knew the answer even before Emily began transforming: not the gross shape-shifting of the townspeople, but something subtler.

'Werewolves can't swim through rapid water,' Emily said. 'And nor can vampires . . .'

Her eyes darkened, a red and glittering star appearing in the centre of each. And her teeth slid further out from her gums, thinning to needle points. She licked her lips with a blackening tongue.

'Oh, Beech, if only there had been more time to explain . . .'

'Keep away from me!' I screamed.

Emily stepped away.

'They will be here in a minute,' she said softly. 'I can save myself. But you, Beech . . . What will you do?'

I looked frantically back towards Smallwood and saw the shadows seething, the darkness torn by growling and snarling.

And just a few metres from me – something I'd only ever read about in comics and watched in late-night films. Yet she was real, standing there, waiting. And I found I wasn't that scared after all.

'My kind,' Emily whispered, moving towards me, 'always hurt their kind. So you have to decide, don't you, what it is you want to do . . .'

The werewolf pack was much nearer now, much louder. They wouldn't kill me, I knew. It was Emily they were after, still waging their ancient war.

The moon came out from behind speeding clouds.

'I've decided,' I answered, holding my hand out towards her.

RIDING THE SILVER WAVE
by Benbow

Midnight, and Craig was at the window again. He was standing in the shadows, just staring out at the ocean.

'He scares me, Dad,' I whispered. 'He's there every night.'

I had shaken our dad half awake and told him to come quick. Now he stood at the door, his face all crumpled up with sleep. 'What's the daft beggar doing?' he growled.

'He's asleep,' I said. 'It's always the same. He sees something out there – something bad.'

Craig sucked in his breath. His blank eyes fixed on the waves somewhere just off the beach, near the jagged rocks of Cove Bay Point.

I crept over to stand beside him and looked out.

The moon was big and fat, almost full. Below our shack, beyond the dunes and the bushes of Three-cornered Jacks, I could see the beach. The sand gleamed like silver. The sea was spread wide and black. The waves were rolling in like always, only now their crests were foaming with moonlight.

'Look out!' Craig shouted and made me jump. 'He'll never make it – no way.'

'Who is it, Craig?' I asked. 'Who can you see?'

'He's got to cut back! Cut back!' Craig said. He was sweating now. 'He's taking the drop. It's suicide. He'll wipe out in the tube!' His eyes flicked, dancing from wave to wave. He gripped the windowsill, knuckles bone-white. 'Watch out for the rocks! The rocks! Noooooooooooooooooooo!' He staggered back.

'It's OK!' I said.

Craig seemed to feel my touch on his arm. He turned, but I could tell he couldn't see me. His stare just went right through, as if I wasn't there. Then he just shuffled away and got back into bed.

'Why does he do that, Dad?' I asked.

Dad scratched the stubble on his chin. 'I reckon the sun's got to him, Josh,' he said.

But as I lay in bed and stared up at the ceiling, I decided it was true what the others said. They said Craig had lost it. They said he was scared, and he had been like that ever since Johnny-boy had died.

★　　★　　★

I felt the pull of the wave long before it reached me. I had counted in six already. They were coming in sets of seven, and I knew the seventh would be the biggest. Craig had taught me that.

In front of me, I could see the beach. To my left, the jagged rocks of Cove Bay Point. Behind, the sparkling blue wave I was going to ride.

This was the big one and I was all knotted up inside. Craig had warned me about the power of a big wave. How it could look good, but curl in early and smash you onto the rocks. How it could suck you down and take you far out to sea — just like the one which had taken Johnny-boy.

They had been mates, him and Craig. The best surfers in Cove Bay, everyone said. But when I asked Craig about it, he just looked away. He said Johnny-boy was crazy, and told me not to listen to what the other surfies said.

But I had heard the talk in Happy Larry's Café. I had heard the rumours about the Silver Wave. The wave that came at night and only on the full moon tide. It was a ghost wave, they said, and only a fool or the devil would dare to take the drop on it.

But that hadn't stopped Johnny-boy. He had gone out to ride it alone. He wanted to prove he was the best and that he wasn't scared of anything. They never did find his body.

I shivered even though the Aussie sun was hot on

my back as I lay floating on my surfboard. But I couldn't back out now. Ratso and his mates were watching me.

They said I wouldn't do it as they watched me stripe my face blue and yellow with zinc sun block – war paint we called it – they said I was chicken, like Craig. But I was about to prove them all wrong.

The seventh wave came in with a rush. I could feel the power of it sucking at the long, leaf-shaped board beneath me. I watched the water rise up behind me into a sparkling mountain of blues and greens, and the foam on the top looked like snow.

I paddled forward with both hands, then the wave scooped me up. It pushed me forward, faster and faster. I gripped the sides of my board and jumped up, tucking my legs in quickly. My feet slapped on the flat of the board. And I was standing – wobbling a lot, maybe, but standing all the same – riding the wave like a sea spirit.

Then, suddenly, the wave just swallowed me up like a giant mouth. It sucked me down and rolled me around its bubbling green tongue. I tumbled round and round, then it spat me out as if I didn't taste good. I hit the bottom and felt all the air bubble out of me. My nose and mouth filled with salty water. After that, I was just rolling, rolling, rolling, until I thought I would never stop.

I crawled out and spat what felt like an ocean onto the sand. 'What a wipe out!' I gasped, glad that my surfboard was still attached to my ankle by its plastic leash.

Craig had seen what had happened. 'You crazy idiot!' he said. 'You're not good enough for a wave that big.'

I could see Ratso and the others laughing and pointing.

'Leave it out, Craig!' I said. 'Just 'cos you're too scared to go out any more, doesn't mean I can't!' I didn't mean to say it, it just sort of came out. I could see I'd hurt him.

'You think you know everything, don't you, Josh?' he said. 'But you don't!'

I had heard it all before, so I picked up my surfboard and stomped off.

'And stay away from Ratso, he's bad news!' I heard him call after me.

Now he was even telling me who my friends should be.

'Is Craigie playing nursie to his baby brother again?' Ratso jeered as I passed. The others thought that was dead funny.

'Shut it, Ratso!' I hissed.

'You gonna make me?' he said, then smiled and he shook his head. 'Na! I forgot you're chicken like your brother!'

'You take that back!'

Ratso's mates surrounded me. Five against one. It didn't look good. I had to think fast.

'Crack-a-can!' I said.

Ratso grinned. 'Are you challenging *me*?'

I nodded. 'Crack-a-can. Half an hour. Happy Larry's Café,' I said. 'Then we'll see who's chicken.'

Ratso's mates danced about with excitement.

'You'll be sorry!' Ratso said and laughed.

'He's always saying stuff like that about us,' I told Craig, as I stashed my board back at the shack.

Craig sat on the steps and looked out at the sea. 'Who cares what he thinks?' he said. 'Just let it go.'

That made me mad. 'What's happened to you, Craig? You used to be so cool. You used to be the best. Now you're—' I couldn't say it. I couldn't put in words the disappointment I felt inside.

I pulled on an old T-shirt and my jeans, and grabbed my bike. Whatever Craig was – or wasn't – it didn't make me the same, I had decided. I would prove I wasn't scared of anything, and I would do it as many times as I needed to. That was why I rode down to Happy Larry's Café that day. That was why I promised to ride the Silver Wave.

I took the short cut down Seagull Avenue and left my bike by the door. Happy Larry's Café was fuller than usual by the time I arrived. Word about my challenge had got around.

'What's going on?' Happy Larry growled, polishing the top of his counter with a dirty rag. He didn't look happy at all.

34

Ratso was waiting, sitting at the table in the corner.

'Who's going to be ref?' I asked, sitting down opposite him.

'Danny,' he said, nodding towards a girl with dark hair.

I nodded. Danny was OK.

Danny put the six cans of Coke on the table and the crowd went quiet. She chose one and held it up so everyone could see. Then she started shaking it. She shook and shook, until we all knew it would explode like a bomb if it was opened. Then she put it back on the table and started switching the cans around. She muddled them all up good and proper, until no-one knew which one was which.

'You know the rules,' Ratso said. 'Whoever gets the bomb has to skull all of them, then we—'

'I know what happens then,' I said, trying to sound as tough as one of those poker players I had seen in old Westerns.

'Six to one chance!' Danny said to the crowd.

Ratso chose first. He picked a can, held it in front of his face and pulled the ring on the top. *Crack! Pfsst!*

He grinned. 'Now let's see if you're as chicken as your brother.'

'Five to one,' Danny called out the odds.

I didn't hesitate, just reached out and chose. I lifted the can to my face. *Crack! Pfsst!*

Everyone relaxed, murmuring and shuffling their feet.

The smile faded from Ratso's face. The odds were getting worse. He had a one in four chance of picking the bomb. His hand hovered over one can for a moment, then he chose another. Everyone crowded in as he held it to his face. *Crack! Pfsst!* He blew out a sigh and grinned.

'I'm no chicken,' I said as Danny called the odds out at three to one. I picked a can and held it to my face, but before I cracked it I said, 'And I'll prove it by riding the Silver Wave.' Then I closed my eyes. *Crack! Pfsst!*

You could have heard a moth sneeze after that. They all just stared at me, mouths open. It was Ratso who broke the silence.

'You know what happened to Johnny-boy,' he said, quietly, 'and he was the best.'

I nodded. I knew.

Ratso was sweating now. 'It comes on the full moon tide – that's tonight.'

'I said I would do it,' I snapped. 'Now you crack a can!'

Ratso just stared at me across the table, a weird look in his eyes. Then, as if in a dream, he reached out and chose one of the two remaining cans. He lifted it to his face slowly. His finger hooked into the metal ring on the top and he closed his eyes.

We waited.

'That's enough!' Happy Larry said, bursting through the crowd suddenly. He snatched the can away from Ratso.

Crack! Pfsst! Ratso's finger caught in the ring-pull.

'I've warned you lot about this before,' Happy Larry boomed, but he never did get the chance to throw us all out.

The can shook in his huge hand. He looked at it and frowned. Then a great gush of Coke whooshed up into the air as the bomb exploded. Up it came and kept coming, jetting out through the hole in the top. Most of it hit him smack in the face.

And suddenly we were all piling out of Happy Larry's Café and running in every direction. I jumped on my bike, but Ratso blocked my way.

'Not so fast, big mouth!' he said. 'If you are going to ride the Silver Wave you'd better be at Cove Bay Point by midnight.'

'I'll be there,' I said.

'And I'll be waiting.'

I woke suddenly. The light from the full moon was streaming into my face through a gap in the curtains. I sat up. Craig's bed was empty, the sheets crumpled and thrown back.

'Craig!' I whispered. He didn't answer.

I slipped out of bed and over to the window. Below, the sea was frothing and foaming in the moonlight. The dark waves crashed onto the beach, driven by the wind and the full moon tide. Then I saw Ratso. He was just a shadow against the silver sand, but I could see he had his surfboard tucked under his arm.

I changed into my shorts and let myself out of the shack as quietly as the squeaky door would let me. I picked up my surfboard and sprinted for the beach. The tough grass whipped my legs and the sand was icy cold under my feet as I ran.

'Thought you'd chickened out,' Ratso said, as I scrambled over the last dune.

He was standing at the water's edge, the wind whipping his hair about and his eyes glowing with that weird light again.

The sea was dark and ugly. A wave roared in and the foam rushed up around my ankles. I felt the cold, and suddenly I was scared. Dead scared.

'Maybe we should just forget all about it,' I said.

I glanced over my shoulder nervously. The dunes were lumpy with shadows. I could see our shack in the moonlight. It was dark, like the others along the beach front. Only the streetlight in Seagull Avenue shone out in the night.

'It's too late to back out now,' Ratso said. He splashed out, lay on his surfboard and began paddling with both hands. He ducked through a wave then bobbed up on the other side.

'What's going on?' a voice asked suddenly. It was Craig. He must have seen us from the shack. He came sliding down a sand dune in a shower of sand and shook me by my shoulders.

'It's Ratso,' I said. 'He's gone out to ride the Silver Wave.'

Craig's face went very pale. 'I've got to stop him,' he gasped, 'before it's too late.'

He ran into the water and plunged into a wave. I just stood there and watched, not knowing what to do. Then I lost him and I wondered if I should follow or go for help. Ratso had vanished too. I panicked. I thought they had both drowned, then suddenly the waves parted and I saw them: Craig thrashing through the water; Ratso too far out and in trouble.

I didn't think twice after that. Craig was going to need all the help he could get and I knew it. I flung myself onto my board and paddled as fast as I could, but I was only halfway out when I saw Ratso go under. A wave rolled over me and I came up just in time to see Craig pull him up again. Then another wave hit me and I lost sight of them.

I suppose I should have known. I suppose I should have realized something was very wrong when I saw the boy sitting cross-legged on his board. The waves didn't seem to touch him. He was drifting through them like they weren't even there. But he had his back to me so I couldn't see him properly. It was only when I was closer that I noticed how thin and skinny he was. Only then did I notice his hair was like plaited seaweed and that his surfboard was glowing electric blue in the water.

I called out. He turned slowly. Then I saw his face, and screamed.

No eyes. No skin. No lips. Just grinning teeth and bone. A white skull face. Dead, but alive.

'You want to ride the Silver Wave with me?' the boy with the skull-face asked. He pointed a bone finger out to sea.

Then I saw it – a monster of a wave rolling towards me. It sparkled with moonlight as if it was made of diamonds. A moving mass of silver, solid yet silent. A ghost wave. And as I watched, I knew I would never escape it.

I turned back towards the shore, but it was too late. The wave reared up behind me. I paddled like crazy, my board cut through the water under me, but it caught me easily. Then suddenly I knew what I had to do.

I gripped the sides of my board and jumped up. My feet slapped on fibreglass, and I was standing. I didn't have time to think, I just did everything automatically. I shifted my weight, angling my board into the wave, and felt the wind on my face as I skimmed across the silver water.

Just for one moment, I thought I could ride the wave and beat it. Then I looked up and saw the water begin to curl in over my head. It came right over until it formed a sparkling tube – a pipe of pure silver – with me racing down the middle.

At the end, ragged, jagged rocks waited like big black teeth foaming in a sea of spit. I knew they would chew me to bits if I hit them, but I couldn't escape. I could only go faster and faster down that tube of death.

Then all of a sudden, out of the middle of the wave came the boy with the skull face. A hole just opened up in the water and out he shot, crouching on his board. He was glowing like a neon sign, his seaweed hair flying in the wind. He grinned at me and surfed alongside for what seemed like a million years. Then he cut straight in front of me, slicing right across the point of my surfboard.

I felt a shudder as the fins on the underside of his board slashed deep into mine. After that I was going down, but before I went under I saw him surf on. He shot through the rocks as if they weren't even there and disappeared in a blinding flash of light. I saw him do it before I went under.

I struggled at first, then I just sank until I hit the bottom. A stream of bubbles blew out of my mouth and burst into a million coloured stars. The stars spun around in front of my eyes, then changed into starfish. Above, I could see the moon, and the waves racing towards the shore. I could imagine the sting of the salt and the howl of the wind. But down below, everything was quiet and calm.

I think I would have stayed there for ever if someone hadn't pulled me up. I'm sure we went up

together, but I broke the surface alone. After that, I remember the waves tossing me about and being thrown onto the sand like a piece of old driftwood. Then everything went dark.

Craig let the sand trickle through his fingers and blow away in the breeze.

We were sitting on a sand dune, looking out at the rocks of Cove Bay Point. Two days had passed since they had pumped the water out of me.

'It was him, wasn't it?' I said.

He nodded without taking his eyes off the sea. The water was blue now and the rocks weren't like teeth any more.

'I have never told anyone this,' Craig said in a quiet voice, 'but it was my fault Johnny-boy died.'

My heart started thumping. 'How do you mean?'

He looked at me with sad eyes. 'I let him go out alone. I couldn't stop him. He just kept saying if he rode the Silver Wave it would prove he was the best. So I waited here on the beach. Then I saw him hit the rocks, but I couldn't help him . . .'

And suddenly it all made sense: the bad dreams, the way Craig had been acting – everything.

'It wasn't your fault,' I said. 'You can't blame yourself.'

We sat in silence for a long while after that, just watching the waves roll in. Then Craig stood up and brushed the sand off his shorts.

43

'Johnny-boy saved me from the rocks,' I said, pointing to the deep scratches across the point of my surfboard.

'I guess so,' he said.

'Maybe it was his way of saying *you* were right and he was wrong,' I said. 'Maybe his ghost is out there somewhere, ready to stop anyone else making the same mistake as him.'

He thought for a moment, then he did something I had not seen him do for a very long time – he smiled.

Craig won an award for saving Ratso's life, which was good because, apart from anything else, it shut Ratso up. And the bad dreams stopped after he told Dad and the others about Johnny-boy. No-one blamed him for what had happened.

Me, I learned what I should have known all along: that my brother was the best, and that sometimes it takes more guts to say *no*.

As for Johnny-boy, nobody knows if his ghost still guards those rocks on Cove Bay Point. So if you want to find out for sure – and you dare – you will just have to ride the Silver Wave yourself.

THE FRIENDSHIP NECKLACE
by Emily Smith

That term, all the girls in Tamsin's class had a craze for friendship bracelets. Suddenly everyone seemed to be making them for everyone else. Jo made one for Tracey in her favourite colours, pink and purple, and Tracey made one for Jo in Rasta colours.

Kaylie made a different one every week, depending who the current best friend was.

Tamsin was not anyone's best friend. But she would probably have been given a bracelet too, if it hadn't been for Werna.

She arrived nearly halfway through the term, a slight, dark-haired girl. Tamsin watched as Mrs Mays introduced her, and decided she was youngish for the class. But suddenly she looked straight out over the room – and Tamsin changed her mind. The pale tense face she was looking at wasn't young at all. It was somehow . . . old.

Mrs Mays spoke brightly – almost too brightly. 'Now, class, I want you all to welcome Werna and help her find her way around.'

There was silence. Even Kaylie, who usually loved showing new people around and bossing them, said nothing. And Tamsin realized that it wasn't just her who thought there was something strange about the new girl. Everyone did. She looked again at the white face, the hollow cheeks, the deep watchful eyes. And then she looked away.

Mrs Mays' was a big class, and Tamsin's table was right the other side from Werna's. So for two days she had no contact with the newcomer. Then one morning, when Tamsin was doodling on the side of her book report, she became aware of a strange feeling – as if someone was looking at her.

She raised her head – and met Werna's dark gaze. For a second or two they stared at each other. And then Werna gave a little nod, as if to say, 'Yes, you'll do.' And Tamsin felt a shiver run down her spine . . .

Just as she was going out of the school gates that afternoon, someone grabbed her arm. Hard.

She spun round indignantly – and found herself staring deep into Werna's eyes. The angry words died on her lips.

'Tamsin.' Werna bent towards her, and spoke quietly. 'You're going to be my friend, Tamsin.'

'Am I?' asked Tamsin. Her voice sounded high, even to herself.

'Yes,' said Werna. 'You're the one.'

'The one?'

'The one to be my friend. The others—' Werna let go of Tamsin's arm to wave a dismissive hand. 'You're the one,' she repeated. Then a strange expression crossed Werna's face. 'Friends are very important to me. Remember that, Tamsin.'

Suddenly she was gone, walking quickly away down the street. Tamsin gazed after her for a moment, then crossed the road to her bus-stop, going over the conversation in her head. It had been . . . well, weird, hadn't it? She ought to feel flattered, really. Usually she'd be pleased that someone wanted to be her friend. But what a strange way to do it. As if . . . as if Werna had made her decision, and she had had no say in the matter at all.

The next day Tamsin kept her head down at her table, careful not to meet Werna's eye. But there was no escape at break-time. As she walked into the playground, she heard the voice. 'Tamsin!' It sounded more of an order than a greeting.

She turned. 'Yes?'

Werna jerked her head towards a far corner. 'There – come over there!'

'Why?' Tamsin burst out. 'Why should I?'

'Because you're my friend.' Werna narrowed her eyes. 'And I need—' She broke off and turned. And somehow – Tamsin didn't quite know how – she found herself following.

'OK then,' said Werna, as they reached the railings. 'Now I want you to tell me.'

They looked at each other in silence. 'Tell you what?' said Tamsin.

A smile crossed Werna's face. 'I want to know about you. All about you. And this school. And the people in our class. Everything.'

'Well, I'll tell you what I can,' said Tamsin uncomfortably.

So she started. She told her about Mum, and Mum's job at the shop, and about Dad having left. And then she told her about the people at school. She started telling her about Philip being a good swimmer and things like that, but Werna didn't want to hear those. She wanted the sad things – the parents' divorces, the friends who had rowed, the boy who found schoolwork more and more difficult each term . . .

That was a Friday, and Tamsin hoped against hope that Werna would leave her alone the following week. But she had just started talking to Philip at break on Monday, when she felt a touch on her arm – a touch that felt like an electric shock.

As Werna led her away, she saw a look of surprise on Philip's face.

It soon got around that Tamsin was best friends with the strange new girl. And people began to avoid her – even Jo and Tracey. They gave her sidelong looks, and fell silent when she came up.

Tamsin watched Jo and Tracey compare friendship bracelets – discuss beads and colours and different knots – and felt she could cry. She decided it was her most miserable term ever . . .

One afternoon, as Mrs Mays was fetching something between lessons, there was a sudden shriek in the corner of the classroom. It was Kaylie.

'A spider! A spider!' she screamed.

'A really big one, too!' said one of the boys.

'Ooh, yes!' cried Tracey, joining them. 'Isn't it huge?'

'And those great hairy legs!' said Candida, giggling.

'I've come over all funny!' cried Kaylie.

'I've come over all funnier!' said Tracey.

'Get rid of it!' shrieked Kaylie. 'Someone get rid of it!'

And someone did – Werna. As Tamsin watched, she reached down and grabbed the big brown spider with her bare hand. For a few seconds she held the struggling creature in the air. And then, slowly, deliberately, she brought up her other hand and ripped off a leg. And then another. And then another.

Suddenly the giggling, shrieking girls were silent.

'You didn't have to do that!' said Kaylie uncomfortably.

'That's cruel!' said Candida indignantly.

Werna shrugged, and, taking the mutilated spider to the window, she threw it out.

Just then Mrs Mays came breathlessly in, and told everyone to settle down. It was over.

That term in Mrs Mays' class wasn't a happy one. Things began to disappear – first, little things like erasers, then bigger things, like a torch Philip brought in one day. And somehow the class lost its old friendly feel. Everyone went around in groups ('cliques', Mrs Mays called them), the girls making their friendship bracelets, the boys just mooching. Candida twisted her ankle, falling down the playground steps, and said someone had pushed her, though no-one saw anything. Even work wasn't going well. 'I don't know,' said Mrs Mays, shaking her head in Maths one afternoon. 'You just aren't getting the hang of things this term.'

Tamsin was scribbling her homework at the kitchen table one evening, when Mum suddenly asked how school was.

'OK,' she muttered.

'Seeing much of Tracey?'

'No.'

'Or Jo?'

'No.'

'Mmm,' said Mum. 'That's rather what I gathered from Janice – you know, Tracey's mum.' She broke some spaghetti, and put it in a pan. 'I bumped into her out shopping today.'

Tamsin chewed at her thumbnail.

'She said you spend all your time with that new girl. Werna, I think she said her name was.'

'Mmm,' said Tamsin.

Mum turned from the cooker. 'So what's she like, this Werna?'

Tamsin shrugged. 'OK.'

'OK? Is that all?'

Suddenly Tamsin saw red. 'I told you, Mum – she's *OK*!' she yelled. 'Don't get at me!'

Mum came up and put an arm round her. 'Look, I'm not trying to get at you. I'm worried.'

Tamsin stared down at her ragged science book.

'I'm worried,' said Mum again. 'You don't seem happy. And I'm worried about this friend. She . . . I mean—' Mum broke off, paused, and suddenly began talking very quickly. 'There are some funny rumours going around about Werna's family. They had to move here in a hurry after . . . strange things happened in their old town.' Mum paused. 'I don't think she sounds a good friend for you, Tammy.'

Tamsin dropped her head in her hands. She wanted to tell Mum everything. To tell her that Werna *wasn't* a good friend. That she made her tell things. That . . . that she frightened her. But somehow – perhaps a memory of those dark, all-seeing eyes – she just couldn't.

One afternoon Werna had to stay on after school

51

to talk to Mrs Mays. The next day she was in a terrible mood.

'I've got to get my own back,' she murmured, glowering up at the classroom window.

'Your own back?' Tamsin followed her gaze. 'On who?'

'Mrs Mays,' said Werna.

'Mrs Mays?' said Tamsin. 'What for?'

Werna narrowed her eyes. 'For what she said to me. For what she said about my work.'

Tamsin bit her lip. 'She's OK, Mrs Mays,' she said slowly. 'A bit strict sometimes, perhaps, but, well—' she shrugged – 'teachers *are*.'

But Werna wasn't listening. 'I'll find out her weakness,' she murmured. 'That's the way. Find her weakness . . .'

It didn't take her long.

'Has anyone been in my desk?' said Mrs Mays one morning, a worried look on her face. 'I had a photo of David at his passing-out parade I brought in to show the staff, and it's disappeared.'

Everyone shook their heads.

'Oh, well,' said Mrs Mays, still looking worried. 'I expect it will turn up.'

The next day was Art. That week's theme was the seaside, and Mrs Mays had brought in some shells and a starfish – 'to inspire you!' as she said.

Tamsin rather enjoyed painting her rock-pool, and was particularly proud of the way she'd done the waving green seaweed. She glanced round at some of the others. Kaylie was painting a mermaid who looked like a Barbie doll, and Philip was doing a pirate ship. Tamsin wondered what Werna was doing over the other side of the room. Art was the one subject Werna was really good at.

'Finish up, now!' said Mrs Mays, about ten minutes before the end of class. 'And I'll come and see what you've done.'

She started going round the room. As she moved to Werna's table, something made Tamsin look up.

What she saw made her heart lurch. Over Mrs Mays' plump kindly face was spreading . . . a look of pure horror. Tamsin saw one hand flutter to her chest, the other push against the table for support. Then slowly, like someone moving in a dream, Mrs Mays walked to the door and out of the classroom.

'Are you all right, Mrs Mays?' Philip called after her. But there was no answer.

Everyone looked at each other in silence. Then Kaylie ran over to Werna's table, then Tracey – then more people.

Suddenly Tamsin was on her feet, too. In a few strides she was there, with the others, looking at Werna's picture.

It was a scene of a beach all right, but not a beach of sunshine and summer holidays. It was a beach of war – of barbed wire and dark skies and wrecked boats – a beach that had just seen a terrible battle.

But now the fighting was over – and all that was left was the dead and injured.

On the bottom right-hand corner, Werna had put a signature letter, 'W'. And next to it, half his chest blown away, lay a young soldier. There was something familiar about the pale features, the blue lifeless eyes, the matted red hair. And Tamsin knew without any doubt that she was looking at the face of David Mays . . .

Her eyes met Werna's. She should say something, she told herself fiercely. She *must*. But she couldn't. She couldn't say a word.

The only person who spoke was Werna. 'See?' she said, triumph mingling with defiance in her voice. And then she was gone.

There were murmurs now. And Tamsin saw people were looking at her. Tracey, Jo, Philip – looking at her, reproach in their eyes. And suddenly she couldn't bear it any more. She tore out of the classroom – away from everyone.

Where could she go? She glanced up and down the corridor. There was no choice. There was only one place to hide – the cloakroom.

It was while she was hiding miserably at the end of the cloakroom that she heard footsteps. She crouched lower behind a dark blue mac.

Someone walked lightly into the room, and stopped. And then there were different, heavier footsteps. Someone else was coming in. As soon as he spoke, Tamsin knew who it was. Philip.

'You just stop it!' Philip's voice was dark with anger. 'You just *stop* it!'

'Stop what?' Another voice Tamsin knew well. So well.

'You know!' said Philip with scorn. 'You *know*! I'm talking about the things you've been doing ever since you got here. Like that thing just now to Mrs Mays. That was . . . cruel!'

Werna gave a low laugh. 'You stupid boy,' she said. 'You don't know what you're talking about!'

There was a short silence. 'Maybe not,' said Philip, 'but I can recognize something . . . bad when I see it. And you've done bad things ever since you came to this school. And I . . . we all want you to stop.'

'And *I* want you to stop interfering,' said Werna angrily. 'And if you don't, I'll get in touch with—' She broke off.

'Yes?' said Philip.

'With your mother,' finished Werna. And Tamsin froze. Philip's mother was dead – everyone knew that. You *never* mentioned Philip's mother. And here was Werna talking about getting in touch with her as cool as anything. And somehow – impossible as it was – there was something that made you think Werna was serious. That it wasn't just a horrible cruel bluff.

After what seemed an age, she heard Philip's voice again.

'You're evil, Werna, that's what you are. Evil!'

And then Tamsin heard footsteps leaving the cloakroom. After a few seconds she rose gingerly to her feet. And came face to face with those dark, nightmare eyes . . .

Just for a second Werna looked startled. And then she smiled. 'Well, hello there, little friend,' she said.

Tell her, Tamsin's mind urged. Tell her – now.

'I'm not!' she said, and her voice seemed to come from a million miles away. 'I'm not your friend. I don't want anything to do with you!'

Werna just looked at her, eyebrows raised.

'He's right!' Tamsin went on, her voice rising. 'He knows what you are! *He* knows!'

Werna continued to stare at her for a moment, and then she spoke. 'My friends are very important to me,' she said slowly.

'I'm not a friend!' Tamsin shouted at her. 'Can't you hear? I'm *not* a friend!'

The eyes weren't dark any longer. They glittered. 'And I don't like it,' Werna went on, 'when friends aren't friends any more . . .'

Tamsin gave a shiver. But she held Werna's gaze. She knew she had to – and somehow she found the strength.

Suddenly Werna was gone. Tamsin sank down upon a bench. She had done it. She had broken Werna's power over her. She really had . . .

For the next few days Werna was not at school. And when she did appear, she didn't look Tamsin's way once. Tamsin felt happier than she'd felt for ages.

On the last day of term, she was just clearing out her drawer, when she suddenly realized someone was standing in front of her. She looked up. It was Werna. She was smiling, and looked really quite . . . ordinary. Tamsin found herself wondering how she'd ever thought she looked strange.

'I've come to say goodbye!' said Werna. 'We're moving on again – I won't be here next term.' She held something up. 'And to give you this. To remember me by.'

Tamsin stared at the loop of woven colours in her hand. 'It looks like a friendship bracelet,' she said. 'Except bigger.'

Werna nodded. 'It's a friendship *necklace*,' she said. 'You wear it round your neck. I made it for you.' She paused, and smiled. 'After all, we *were* friends, weren't we?'

Tamsin took the necklace, and gazed at it. Three colours – black, red and silver-grey – had been evenly woven into a band about a centimetre wide. The necklace had been finished off with a neat knot – Werna was good with her hands.

'It's pretty,' said Tamsin, feeling she ought to say something.

Werna grinned. 'Well, try it on! See if it fits.' She slipped it over Tamsin's head, and cried in triumph.

'Yes, it does!' Then she met Tamsin's eyes. 'You will wear it, won't you?'

Tamsin stared back at her. Something of the old power was at work. 'Yes,' she said. 'Yes, I'll wear it.'

Tamsin let herself into the flat, panting slightly, and flung her stuff on the floor of the hall. It had started as a nice hot day – but now it was beginning to feel close. So close, in fact, that she was beginning to have difficulty breathing.

She went to the kitchen to make herself a glass of orange juice. Perhaps that would make her throat feel less tight.

She sipped the orange slowly, and then wandered back to pick up her things in the hall. No, she decided, she wouldn't do it now. She'd do it later, when Mum had got back. Suddenly she wished Mum was here – but it was no good wishing. Mum wouldn't be back for at least two hours.

Switching on the television, she slumped down in front of a kids' programme. She tried to concentrate, but gradually found her breathing getting more and more difficult. She sat up after a bit, which made it easier – but then it started getting worse again . . .

Breathing hard, Tamsin put her hand to her neck – and felt the friendship necklace. It was no longer loose, but tight on her skin. How had that happened? It had been big enough to go over her head that morning – but now it was fast against her neck.

Fear gripped her. She pulled at the necklace, but it held like an iron band. She fumbled at the knot behind her neck. But that knot was never going to give . . .

Her head was full of the sounds of her lungs gasping, her blood pounding. She was fighting, trying to breathe – fighting whatever it was that was stopping her. But it was too strong – too strong for her.

Now Tamsin was on her feet. She must do something – find something to cut the necklace. The bathroom cabinet – there'd be some scissors in there! Must get down the corridor, *must* get to the bathroom. Somehow she made it. Staggering to the cabinet, she flung the door open and grabbed the scissors. But no – no good, no *good*! She couldn't get the blade under the straining necklace.

Then her eye fell on the packet of razor blades. She snatched one out, and began to hack at the necklace. One, two, three, four. She felt the blood, warm and wet on her fingers, but still the necklace possessed her. And suddenly, over the pounding of the blood in her ears, and the sound of her own desperate gasps for air, she heard a voice. 'My friends are very important to me,' it said. 'I don't like it when friends aren't friends any more.' And then she was falling, falling, falling . . .

*   *   *

Tamsin woke to find herself in bed, in a dimly-lit curtained space. There was something over her mouth – and also something wrapped around her throat.

Mum was beside her, and a nurse stood above, removing the mouth thing. 'There, she's OK now,' said the nurse.

'Oh, Tammy.' Mum pressed her hand. There were tears in her eyes.

'What . . . what happened?' whispered Tamsin.

'You had a terrible asthma attack.' Mum's eyes were wide. 'I mean, we didn't even know you were asthmatic at all. It's all been a most terrible shock. It was lucky I got back early from work to surprise you. Otherwise—' She gulped.

Tamsin stared at her. 'The necklace . . . it . . .'

Mum squeezed her hand. 'Just forget it all, now. You panicked and did something very silly with a razor blade. But you didn't go *that* deep, thank goodness. So the doctors say you'll be all right.'

Three weeks later, bandages off, Tamsin surveyed herself in the mirror at home. She looked at the purplish scar tissue on her neck, and recognized what she saw.

Werna had given her something to remember her by. She said she would, and she had. The four slashes on Tamsin's neck made, clear on her skin, a perfect letter . . . 'W'.

THE WARNING
by Pia Ashberry

Now that it's all over, I've started to think it was a dream. A bad one, mind. Realistic, too. But only a dream. Course, it happened when I was awake and not asleep, so by rights, it were a daydream. But daydreams are England winning the World Cup, or getting a snog off Lisa Bradley. This weren't nothing like that. So I suppose you'd have to call it a waking dream, or a vision, summat like that. Still, whatever, it saved Tom Ferguson's life. And changed mine for ever.

We cornered him behind the science block. Me and my trusted lieutenant, Jamie. There were a couple of scrawny Year Sevens having a fag, but we soon got rid of them. 'Beat it,' I said. 'We've got business to attend to.' We turned our attention to the business. Tom Ferguson, the wimp of Withington High. You know, some people have got a face that is asking for it. Tom's is like that. Dead soft, with these sort of pudgy cheeks, that go all red when anyone speaks to him, and these kind of melty brown eyes that look like someone's drowned his favourite kitten. Makes you want to smash that squidgy face right in. And then there's his accent. That poncy Southern accent that he doesn't even try to hide. Should have stayed in the south with all the other posh boys.

Jamie had him by the scruff of the neck and was pushing his face right into Tom's, like they do in films. I stood back a bit, let him get on with it.

'All right, Tommy. IT'S . . . pay day,' he said.

The wimp started to shake and stutter.

'Pppplease . . . I . . . I . . . haven't got any.'

'Don't take the mick, Ttttommy. Me and Jamie, we don't like it,' I said, dead soft like. 'Cos you know what, to show power – real power, you don't need to shout. That's where Jamie went wrong.

'Don't make things hard for yourself, Tommy,' I said, smiling like we was chummy like. 'Because Jamie here is gonna search you. And if he finds that you're lying to us . . . well, I don't like to think what could happen. Jamie here's an animal, aren't you, Jamie?'

'Rrrraaagh,' growled Jamie, right into Tom's face.

I nearly wet meself laughing. Tom nearly wet himself and all. Not with laughing, though.

Anyway, it did the trick right enough. Tom reaches into his pockets, pulls out a couple of pound coins.

'Here, it's all I've got. My dinner money.'

Jamie let go of his shirt and I walked up and took the money.

'Never mind, Tommy lad, you could do with losing a bit of weight off them fat cheeks of yours.'

I pinched his cheek hard, digging my finger and thumb right into that soft, flabby cheek, twisting them a bit.

'Same time tomorrow, Tommy, then,' I said. 'Only we'll be wanting three pound off you. Me and Jamie, we're growing lads, aren't we, Jamie?'

'Rrrrraaaagh,' growled Jamie and we walked off.

It was that same day, on the way home, that I first saw him. Jamie had got on his bus, and I carried on walking up Carlisle Street, till I got to the crossing. You have to cross there – it's this big dual carriageway, where the cars bomb along. Not even the real hardcases, who like to play chicken – you know, running out in front of the cars – play it on this road. After I pressed the button, I looked around, and there was this kid standing next to me. He seemed to have come from nowhere. A skinny kid, wearing jeans and a torn T-shirt. Which was flipping crazy, seeing as it was the middle of January. Anyway, as I'm staring, he steps off the kerb, just like that, without looking or nothing.

'Watch it,' I shouted, but my voice was swallowed up by the noise of the thundering traffic, and he never looked round. Just carried on walking. I shut my eyes. I didn't want to see the splattered mess he was gonna be. But there was no sound of cars screeching to a halt or swerving to avoid the kid. No sound of crunching bone. I opened my eyes again. I couldn't believe it. He was stood at the other side of the carriageway, staring straight at me. He looked unharmed, but there seemed to be something not right about him – it sounds daft, but something seemed damaged. I was trying to figure out what it was, when a girl came up beside me and pressed the button, even though I'd already done it.

'Flipping headcase,' I said to her. 'Did you see that?'

She looked away without answering, the snotty cow. And when I looked back across the road, the boy was gone.

All that week at school, we got Tom Ferguson's dinner money off him. Then on Friday, a strange thing happened. This theatre company comes into school and does this play about bullying. I didn't want to watch it, but Mrs Hayes, the English teacher,

said we all had to. Anyway, after a bit, I started to enjoy it. Course, I'm not stupid, I knew you were meant to be feeling dead sorry for the girl who was bullied and that. But I didn't. Not really. Not then. I thought she was weak. And you've got to be tough to survive. Besides, the bullies were better characters. They were funny, they got things done. And people were scared of them. After the play, there was this discussion about bullying. I felt weird but I didn't show it. I kept expecting Tom to point at me and say, 'Him over there, him and his mate Jamie, they're bullies.' But nobody said owt. Like I said, people are scared.

But that afternoon, me and Jamie got called into the Head's office.

'Sit down,' she said, after the secretary had let us in. We sat in the two chairs opposite her desk, strewn with papers. She carried on sorting through them, ignoring us, making us sweat.

'I've been hearing some disturbing news about you two,' she said finally.

'Who, us, Miss?' said Jamie.

'I've heard reports that you've been using threatening behaviour to extort money from other children.'

'That's not true, Miss,' I said. 'We wouldn't do anything like that.'

'I hope not,' she said coldly. 'Because you're both bright lads, and I wouldn't want to see you jeopardizing your futures, or the image of the school.

This school does not have bullying. Do I make myself clear?'

'We're not bullies, Miss,' I said. 'Honest.'

'You'd better not be,' she said, glaring at us with her bulging, fish eyes. 'Now get back to class. I haven't got time for this.'

We left her office; started to walk slowly back. I was fuming. I couldn't believe that he'd had the nerve to go against me like that.

'How do you think she knew?'

'How do *you* think, you big thickhead. Little Tttommy Tttucker. Well, I tell you what, Jamie, we're gonna make him sing for his supper.'

'But the Head . . .'

'So what? She's not gonna hear about it, Jamie. We'll make sure of that.'

We walked back through reception and past the toilets. 'Just a sec,' said Jamie, going in. I carried on walking along the silent corridor – Jamie could catch me up. And then I saw him. As I turned the corner into the language block, there he was. Tom Ferguson. Right in front of me. I couldn't believe my luck. Not that I was going to do anything. Not then. Not in school. I was going to warn him, that's all, of what he had coming. I speeded up and he did the same. I didn't know whether he'd seen me or not. He hadn't looked round. I speeded up some more – I was almost running now. And then he stopped. This is it, I thought to myself, planning what I was going to say. Then he turned round, and I nearly threw up right there and then. It wasn't Tom. How could I have ever thought it was? It was the kid, the skinny kid from the crossing on Carlisle Street. And his face . . . his face was all wrong – I can't explain it properly, but it was like it had been put on at the wrong angle or something. Like it was crooked. His eyes were strange too, not blank exactly, but sort of without expression. As if the worst thing possible had happened and he'd accepted it.

I tried to pull myself together.

'Hey, kid,' I said. 'What you been doing to yourself? You look like Dracula.'

The kid said nothing, just started to walk towards me. I stood my ground – you can't show you're scared, and besides, he couldn't have been more than eleven.

'Wait for me, Pete.'

Jamie's familiar voice drifted along the corridor. I turned around, and when I turned back, the skinny kid was gone. I ran to the end of the corridor, looked up the next one, but he was nowhere to be seen.

'What's the matter with you?' said Jamie, catching me up.

'Where did he go?' I asked.

'Where did who go?'

'The kid, the kid with the funny eyes.'

'What you on about? What kid?'

I stared at Jamie but he wasn't joking, he hadn't

seen him. I laughed and pretended that I was having him on, but I felt like I was going mad. I knew there must be a rational explanation, but I couldn't think of one. How could Jamie not have seen him? The whole thing was totally weird.

The day had gone from bad to worse, and it was all one person's fault. Tom Ferguson's. The thought of getting him cheered me up no end. When the bell rang, we made sure we were the first out, and waited by the school gates. We wouldn't do him there. We'd follow him, wait till we got to a nice, quiet spot and then go for it. Wrapped up in my beautiful thoughts of revenge, I never saw them. Jamie did, though. He nudged me.

'You're not gonna believe this,' he said.

'What?' I asked, looking in the direction he was pointing at.

Tom Ferguson was walking towards the school gates, surrounded by a group of kids from our class. Not his friends, mind. He didn't have any friends. Mostly, they were our friends.

'Joe Redmond, what do you think you're doing?' I said to one of them as they passed by.

'We're walking Tom home,' he said, smiling smugly.

The group turned together to the right and moved off down the road. There were too many of them to scare off.

'Don't worry,' I said to Jamie. 'They'll soon get

bored. You watch. In a week, they'll have for-
gotten all about that stupid play. And then we'll
get him. Even if we have to wait all term, we'll get
him.'

That night, I dreamt about the skinny kid. He was
standing in my bedroom, watching me as I slept. His
face was oozing blood and pus – it was dripping all
over the carpet. His right arm was dangling like a
dummy's arm, and at the elbow, the bone was jutting
out. He walked towards me, his dead arm swaying
stupidly. He raised his hand and began to wipe his
face with it. Then he began to wipe his bloody hand
onto my face and in my hair. I woke up, sat up,
reached for the light by the bed. I could feel the
beads of sweat dripping down from my upper lip and
my temples. Sweat! I leapt out of bed and towards
the mirror. Please, God, I thought, let it be sweat. I
looked at my face in the mirror. Not a drop of blood
in sight. It really was only a dream.

All week they followed Tom about like flipping
bodyguards. The whole class seemed to be taking
turns. There was no way we could get to him. Funny
thing was though, you would have thought it would
have made him feel all important and pleased with
himself. It didn't, though. If anything, he looked
more miserable and scared than usual. I suppose he
knew that good intentions don't last for ever. And

that sooner or later, we were going to get him.

It happened sooner. The second week after the play. On the Monday. I had a good feeling when I saw Stacy and Caroline come out on their own. They didn't even notice me and Jamie by the gates. Too busy nattering about some party they'd been to. Then came a whole group of lads from our class. They were off for a game of footy in the park. Even asked if we wanted to play. Tom Ferguson wasn't with them. He wasn't with Gina Brook either, nor Susan Wheel. Nor anybody. The whole class had come out now, and he wasn't with any of them. I turned to Jamie.

'You don't think we could have missed him, do you?'

Jamie smiled and shook his head. 'No chance,' he said and pointed towards the school. Tom Ferguson was walking slowly towards us.

We followed him without saying a word. It meant that he had to keep looking round to check we were still there. He was trying not to, you could tell. But he couldn't help the little glances over his shoulder. We kept the exact same distance, never too near, never too far. He didn't run, though, or even speed up. Just kept walking at the same pace.

He turned down Rosamund Street. It was the same way that me and Jamie walked. Rosamund Street was where the bus station was, where Jamie usually got his bus. If Tom got on a bus, we'd have to leave it.

I had no idea where he lived, and I didn't want to go miles out of the way. Still, it didn't matter that much. There was always tomorrow, and besides, we'd given him a right scare, following him like this.

He didn't get on a bus. He weaved his way across the aisles where the buses stood to the other side and started up Carlisle Street. Couldn't have been better. Now, if anyone accused us of following him, I could say it was my way home. He walked up to the crossing and pressed the button. Me and Jamie followed and stood behind him. And this time, he turned right round, looked me straight in the eye. And there was something in that look. It wasn't fear, or begging or nowt like that. I dunno why but something about it made me feel scared, not of him, of . . .

And then something really weird happened. He went completely still. Like a statue. Like he was frozen in time. I waved my hand in front of his face. Nothing, not a flicker. I looked round at Jamie, but he looked the same. He was frozen, too. And then I saw him. On the other side of the carriageway, the skinny boy running towards the crossing. And chasing him, a group of lads, big lads, shouting and laughing.

'Steve's gonna have a nasty accident,' they were chanting, like a football chant.

There were six of them, six on one. Why didn't anyone stop them? I thought. But there was no-one else around. And there was no way I could get across, not unless the lights changed. He was at the crossing now, but he didn't press the button. The knot in my stomach tightened. I knew what he was going to do. He looked around at the boys running, he looked at the cars bombing past, and then stepped off the kerb. I closed my eyes and prayed for the lights to change. But I knew they hadn't.

When I opened my eyes, the other boys had gone. But the skinny kid was still there, on the opposite side, a trickle of blood running down his cheek. He started to beckon. To me? Was he beckoning to me? Then I remembered Tom. Tom. He wasn't frozen any more. He was standing right at the edge of the kerb about to . . . oh my God, about to . . . I looked at Jamie, but he didn't seem to realize what was happening. It was up to me. I lunged forward, threw my arms around Tom. He wrestled against me, trying to pull away, but I was stronger. I yanked him hard, and we both fell to the ground, him on top of me. I rolled out from underneath him.

'Did you see him?' I panted. 'The boy. Did you see him?'

Tom looked confused. 'What?' he asked.

I looked at Jamie, asked him. He shook his head. 'What's going on?' he asked.

I got to my feet, and held out my hand towards Tom to pull him up.

'I'm sorry,' I said. 'I'm really sorry.'

He looked at me, gobsmacked. Then, I dunno why, he held out his hand, let me help him up.

'You know, for a second there, just a second,' he said, 'I thought I did see . . .'

'What?' I asked urgently.

'Nothing,' said Tom. 'It was nothing.'

'I'm sorry,' I said again. 'For everything.'

Jamie looked from me to Tom.

'What the hell's going on?' he asked.

Jamie thinks I've lost my bottle. Either that, or I've gone off my head. He leaves Tom alone, though – he'd have me to answer to if he didn't. But he doesn't believe in the kid; doesn't understand what nearly happened. I'm not sure I do either. But like I said before, whatever the kid was – ghost, premonition, or hallucination, he saved Tom Ferguson's life. And changed mine for ever.

THE FACE
by Paul Stewart

Ben woke with a start and sat bolt upright in bed. Shivers of cold dread ran up and down his spine. He glanced round at his clock. It was that no-time-at-all dead of midnight, with all the zeros showing on the digital display. As if to confirm it, the bells were chiming outside. Not that they had woken him – Ben was used to living so near to the church. No. It had been something quite different. A scratching sound; muted and muffled, though no less insistent for that.

Ben cocked his head to one side and listened. But the scratching was gone.

'I must have dreamt it,' he said, as he twisted round to plump up his pillow.

At that moment, there was a click and a whirr,

followed by a rattling flap-flap-flap. Ben spun round. His heart was pounding.

The cause of the sudden noise was instantly apparent. The catch on his roller-blind had given way and the whole lot had shot upwards, and spun noisily to a standstill.

'Is that all it was?' he said, with a grin. 'I th—'

As he had spoken, so he had lowered his eyes. Suddenly his gaze focused, and he found himself staring at the face.

Ben yelped with terror and his heart started beating more furiously than ever. He couldn't scream, he couldn't breathe – yet neither was he able to turn away.

Pressed against the glass, the face was hideously distorted. One bulging eye glared at him wildly, the other had all but disappeared behind the flattened cheek, while the nose was squashed, bloodless white, to the side. As Ben continued to stare, rigid with fear, so the twisted mouth began to move.

'One-two,' it moaned. 'One-two, one-two.' With every repetition, the voice sounded more desperate than before, while the face itself turned an ever-deepening shade of purple.

Abruptly, the counting stopped altogether. But though silent, the mouth slowly mimed one final word. Ben watched grimly as the swollen tongue brushed the back of the teeth, and the lips pursed together for an instant. There was no doubt as to the identity of that word.

'*Help?*' he whispered. 'But how?'

But there came no answer. The face had disappeared. Ben didn't know whether to laugh or cry. He was relieved, but the remnants of his terror remained. His palms were wet, his mouth was dry and, as he tied the cord of the broken blind to the radiator under his window, his fingers were shaking uncontrollably.

Two questions echoed round his head. Where had the face come from? And where had it gone?

As Ben woke and looked blearily round his room, the events of the previous night came flooding back. Now, however, with the sun shining and the birds singing, it seemed most likely that he had simply had a particularly unpleasant nightmare.

On the other hand, the blind *was* broken, and as he went to untie it from the radiator, Ben hesitated. He realized his fingers were trembling again.

'Go on,' he said impatiently. 'There's nothing there.'

Thankfully he was right. At least, nothing that shouldn't have been. Just the garden, the garage, the back gate. Ben smiled. Everything was back to normal.

Padding down the landing to the bathroom, Ben heard his dad humming something tuneless in his bedroom; the twins arguing in theirs; his mum downstairs clattering around in the kitchen – the wonderfully ordinary sounds of just another Saturday morning.

It was while washing his face that Ben sensed that something *out of* the ordinary was once again intruding. With his head down over the basin, soapy flannel in hand, he paused. The hairs at the back of his neck were standing on end. Something was wrong.

'Don't be daft!' Ben muttered. 'It's nothing.'

But even as he spoke, he heard the squeaky, scrabbling sound of scratching once again – like frantic rat claws; like nails scraping down a blackboard.

'It's just your imagination,' Ben told himself.

The noise, however, would not be reasoned away. Scratch, scratch, scratch, it went. Scratch. Scratch. Scratch.

Slowly, Ben raised his head. Not that he wanted to, but he couldn't *not* look up. He had to see what was there. If it was the face again, then he hadn't had a nightmare the previous night. Or rather, he *had* – but he'd been awake at the time!

Finally, looking straight ahead of him, Ben saw that the hot water had steamed up the mirror. He tutted nervously, lifted his hand and began wiping away the condensation where the reflection of his face should have been. The next instant, Ben froze.

'NO!' he gasped.

For there it was again: the face that Ben hoped he had only dreamt about. Crushed against the inside of the glass and distorted further by the water on the mirror, it looked more monstrous than ever. Ben stared in horror. The bulging eye was criss-crossed with a network of broken veins − like a scoop of raspberry ripple ice cream; the mouth was blue, cracked, pleading.

'One-two. One-two,' it moaned with awful predictability.

'Who are you?' Ben cried out. 'What do you want?'

Again, Ben's questions went unanswered, as the lips mimed their silent plea for help.

'But I don't know what to do!' Ben said desperately. There was a lump in his throat, and tears of fear and frustration were welling up in his eyes. 'Tell me. Tell me,' he sobbed. 'Just tell me!'

But the face could not tell Ben anything more. It had fallen still; ominously still. As Ben continued to stare, he knew that the mouth had stopped breathing and that the eye − though still glaring − could no longer see.

The face was dead.

Ben couldn't eat any breakfast that morning. He wanted to tell someone about the face, but the twins were too young to understand, and he was worried about how his mum would react − she'd probably whisk him off to the doctor's, knowing her. No, Ben knew that he would have to keep the ghost or ghoul, or whatever it was, strictly to himself.

Nevertheless, as he and his mum had traipsed round town looking for a new pair of jeans – button-fly Levi 501s, to be precise – Ben's mum couldn't help noticing that something was up.

'Are you *sure* you're OK?' she said, as they climbed back into the car.

'I told you,' he said. 'I'm fine.'

As he fumbled around for his seat-belt, Ben could feel his mum's eyes staring at him. It was no good trying to fool her. She *always* knew when something was the matter.

'It's just . . . I was thinking of the French test we've got on Monday,' he said.

Ben's mum nodded silently.

'And thanks again for the jeans,' said Ben, looking down at his legs proudly. 'They're brill.' He paused. 'Can I go over to Gary's house when we get back?' he said. 'Show 'em off.'

'If you like,' his mum replied in that clipped voice she reserved for any talk which involved his best friend. 'When you've helped me in with the shopping.'

Mrs Richards didn't approve of Gary Marten. She thought his hair too long, his clothes outrageous, his manners atrocious – and she didn't like the way his parents allowed him to stay up till all hours.

In short, she considered Gary a bad influence.

'Make sure you're back by one, though,' she said. 'And I do *not* want you going to the dump,' she added. 'Ben?' she said, glancing round at the boy. 'Are you listening to me?'

But Ben was not listening. He hadn't heard a single word. He was staring ahead, his white-knuckled hands gripping the seat.

The face was making its third appearance – this time, pressed against the windscreen. Trying his best not to panic, Ben watched intently as the face performed its terrifying routine. He looked at the chewed, scrabbling fingernails, at the smudge of short hair, at the glaring, bloodshot eye.

Who *are* you? he wondered.

There was an angry scratch on the crushed nose. Droplets of blood were smeared on the glass. Angry and frightened, Ben tore his gaze away from the windscreen and looked down into his lap.

'One-two. One-two,' the voice rasped.

'Ben! What is it?' his mum asked anxiously.

But Mrs Richards' concern was lost on her son. Locked inside his private nightmare, Ben was both blind and deaf to everything else. He looked up again.

The face was still once more. Around it was the outline of something rectangular, shiny white, metal – as if the whole hideous scene had been framed.

Slowly, the face faded away, until only the frame remained. The next instant it, too, was gone. Ben gasped, and put his hand to his mouth, to hide his trembling lips.

'Ben?' he heard. His mum's voice sounded worried.

He turned to look at her. He knew that she wouldn't believe he'd been thinking about his French test again. He smiled sheepishly.

'I . . . I just remembered a nightmare I had,' he said. It was as close to the truth as he dared go. 'Horrible, it was.'

Or rather, *is*! he thought with a shudder.

When Ben knocked at the door, he heard Gary inside calling up to his mum.

'We're off down the park, all right?'

'Don't be late for lunch,' Mrs Marten called back.

The door opened, and Gary appeared.

'Watch'er,' he said, and grinned.

Ben's mouth dropped open. The shoulder-length hair that his mum so disapproved of was no more: Ben doubted whether she would like the crew-cut any better.

'Nice pair of jeans,' Gary noted admiringly.

'I got them this morning,' Ben said.

'Yeah, I was in town too,' said Gary.

Ben turned and grinned. 'I noticed,' he said. 'How come you got it cut so short?'

'Oh, I dunno,' Gary shrugged. 'For a laugh!' he said.

Ben smiled. That was so typical of Gary. Everything he did was *for a laugh*! He remembered the time that Gary had sabotaged the school bell; at the end of the first lesson, it sounded as though the entire school was breaking wind. He remembered when Gary had superglued all the toilet doors shut; when he'd got his rabbit drunk; when he'd let down the tyres on the school mini-van. And then, of course, there was the time he'd decided to shoplift. He hadn't chosen sweets or a magazine, of course – not Gary!

'What are we looking for?' said Ben, as he'd followed Gary up and down the aisles of the DIY warehouse.

'I'll know when I see it,' Gary replied.

The next moment he'd stopped in front of a display of huge orange and black packs. A smile crept over his face.

Ben could still remember the thrill of excited terror he'd felt as they'd walked out, bold as brass, past the cash-desk and on to the forecourt carrying the package between them.

'What *are* they?' Ben asked.

Gary had shrugged and looked down at the packing. '*Filmore*,' he read out. 'Disposable Industrial Vacuum-Cleaner Sacks.' He grinned. 'Bumper Pack!'

'But what did you nick *them* for?' Ben had asked.

Gary snorted as he tossed the package into an empty trolley. Then, as now, the answer had been the same. 'For a laugh!' he said.

'Anyway,' he added, as he rubbed his hand over his head, 'it's nice and cool.'

Ben nodded absentmindedly as they headed along the pavement. Something was troubling him. The icy tingles were once again dancing up and down his spine – and he knew what *that* meant.

So far, the face had appeared at his bedroom window, in the bathroom mirror and on the windscreen. Where would it turn up next?

Perhaps it needs glass to materialize, he thought. Or at least something shiny. And if that's the case . . .

Determined not to let his eyes stray, Ben walked on with his head down and eyes glued to the pavement. He passed between all the parked cars and shop windows without once looking up. Only when they reached the park did Ben finally lift his gaze.

He looked all around the park and sighed with relief. The shivers had gone.

As usual, although they'd come to the park, this was not to be Gary or Ben's final destination. Without stopping at the swings or slides, they walked on, past the tennis courts and bowling green, and up to a gap in the railings at the far end.

Ducking down, Ben squeezed through the fence and picked his way through the matted tangle of brambles on the other side. A stray shoot snagged on his sweatshirt for an instant, before snapping back behind him.

'Oy! Careful!' Gary yelled, as the thorny stem slapped viciously into his face.

Ben turned to see Gary wiping away the beads of blood, where the vicious barbs had scraped across his nose.

'You all right?' said Ben. 'I'm sorry, I . . .'

'Yeah, I'm all right,' came the gruff reply. 'Let's just get out of here.'

As the pair of them emerged on the other side, they finally straightened up and looked round. What new delights would the dump have in store for them today?

'Over there,' said Gary, and pointed.

Ben looked. On, under and around an old metal bedstead was a heap of tin cans that definitely had *not* been there the previous week. The two boys went to investigate.

'They're full!' said Gary excitedly as he picked one up, and immediately began shaking it as hard as he could.

'Careful!' Ben shouted. 'They're fizzy. They might explode.'

'Exactly,' said Gary, as he hurled the can at a pile of rubble.

The can burst with a bang, and a shower of frothy orange rained down.

'You have a go,' said Gary.

Ben did as he was told, though reluctantly. He was less reckless than his friend. In fact, if it wasn't for Gary, he'd never come to the dump at all. Now he was there once again, the last thing he wanted was exploding metal slicing into his fingers. On the other hand, Ben was not about to bottle out. He couldn't!

He picked up a can and jiggled it around half-heartedly. In his hand, the orangeade had become a live grenade – minus pin. *Get rid of it! Quick!* his brain commanded. But Ben made a fatal mistake. He glanced down at his weapon.

And there, staring back at him from the silvery base of the can was a face. But not *his* face – this was no reflection. This was *the* face. The bulging eye swivelled round in its socket.

'*AAAAARGGH!*' Ben screamed and flung the can as far away as he could. He hoped it would explode, destroying the terrible face once and for all. But it didn't. It landed with a soft thud on the earth and rolled out of sight among some weeds.

Ben was petrified. What was going on?

'Gary?' he said.

There was no answer. He looked around. His friend had gone.

'Gary!' he said again, louder this time.

Suddenly, Ben felt cold: his teeth chattered, his legs felt wobbly and weak.

'Ga-ry?' he shouted. 'Where *are* you?'

It was just like Gary to be hiding. He was always leaping out from hiding places, making him jump. But this time Ben was worried, and as he looked around the dump, so the face haunted him in all its horrendous detail. The eye, the lips, the tongue, the smear of blood . . . The short hair . . .

'Gary!' Ben gasped. All at once, he knew that it was his friend's face that he had seen — not as he remembered him, but as he looked now. Right now! And if that was the case . . . Ben swallowed nervously.

'GA-RY!!' he screeched.

The nightmare had finally become reality. Ben ran this way and that, frantically searching for his friend before it reached its horrendous conclusion.

'WHERE ARE YOU?' he screamed. 'GARY!!' Please let me find him. Please. 'GARY!!' I promise I'll never, ever, EVER come here again. Or stay out late. Or . . . or . . . anything! Just let him be all right. 'GAAA-RYYY!!!'

The silent reply was unbearable. How long had he been missing? Ben looked at his watch. He trembled with sudden foreboding: it was 12.12. Unable to move a muscle, Ben watched, horrified, as the seconds counted by. 9 . . . 10 . . . 11 . . . 12.

One-two. One-two. One-two.

13 . . . 14 . . .

'I'm too late,' he whispered miserably.

And then he heard it. The most muffled of muffled scratchings. If it hadn't been so familiar, he would never have noticed it at all. Ben spun round. Some way ahead, and tilting to one side, was a rusting chest-freezer. He remembered the curious frame which had surrounded the face. It was white; shiny white . . .

'No,' Ben shuddered.

He raced over, and tried to lift the lid. It was stuck fast.

'Just let me be wrong,' Ben muttered, as he searched round for something to jemmy it open with. 'Let him be somewhere else. Let him be safe.'

Seizing hold of a length of twisted iron, he rammed it into the gap between the freezer and its lid. As rust crumbled away in his hands, Ben thought for an awful moment that the pole was too flimsy to break the lock.

Suddenly, there was a CRACK! and the lid burst open.

Like a jack-in-the-box – a monstrous jack-in-the-box with bulging eyes, purple skin and swollen tongue – Gary's head and shoulders burst from the freezer. He gulped down mouthfuls of the delicious air.

Ben's shock when Gary had appeared had turned to a wonderful sense of relief as he realized that he *had* been able to help after all. But now he was angry; furious.

'You idiot!' he raged. 'You stupid halfwit! Even the twins wouldn't be so moronic as to climb

into an empty fridge or freezer – and they're only five!'

'I know,' Gary wheezed, miserably. 'I was going to . . . to jump out on you . . .'

'For a laugh, eh?' said Ben. 'You could have been *killed*!'

Gary nodded. 'The catch broke,' he said miserably.

He looked down, and from the look in his eyes, Ben knew his friend was reliving the horror of finding himself trapped. 'I couldn't *breathe*, Ben,' he said finally. 'I kept trying to scratch a hole in the seal; to get my lips into the gap, to . . .'

'I know,' said Ben softly.

Gary looked up. 'It's a miracle you found me in time. How did you guess where I was?'

Ben stared back at his friend. He'd had some kind of premonition, that much was clear. But as to how, he hadn't got a clue. He was bursting to tell Gary all about it, but something stopped him. Ben had the feeling – stronger than anything he'd ever felt before – that if he *did* explain what had happened, he would never be allowed to see the future again. And maybe, someday, he would need to. Maybe, someday, he would save someone else's life – perhaps even his own . . .

'Well?' said Gary.

Ben shrugged. It wasn't often that he got the better of his friend, and he wasn't going to miss the opportunity to rub it in. 'Because you're an idiot!'

he said. 'I just looked for the most stupid, the most
dangerous, the most *idiotic* place to hide,' he laughed.
'And there you were!'

FIRST THERE WAS ONE

by Brian Morse

'Sarah—!'

Something in the voice made Alex look up from the comic he was reading, sprawled out on the edge of the lawn.

'What's up?' he asked as Mum ran down the steps and past him.

'Sarah! Stop that! I'm fed up with you always playing that game!'

It's the way girls of her age play, Alex thought as Mum reached his five-year-old sister. They talk to themselves.

Sarah looked up as Mum's shadow fell across her. 'You frightened him away!' She scrambled to her feet. 'You're mean, mean, mean!' She stamped her foot.

'It's time for your television programme.' Mum grabbed Sarah's hand and pulled her when she resisted. 'I'll pick the things up later. Come on. I don't like you out here on your own.'

On your own? Alex thought.

As the television went on full blast inside, he picked himself up, dusted down his jeans and walked over to where Sarah had been playing. There was the usual paraphernalia of a dolls' tea party: plastic cups and saucers and plates, some plastic knives and forks left over from the Christmas party, a bowl of imitation fruit, a toy toaster with two pieces of foam bread inside. Alex prodded the toaster with his toe, trying to turn it the right way up. The bread was stuck. *Frightened him away?* What had Sarah meant by that? *Him? Who?*

A faint, chill puff of breeze blew out of the bushes and across the lawn. Alex shivered. At his feet the toaster gave a loud click and the toast shot out onto the grass. Something he couldn't see scuttled in the dry leaves under the bushes. He could have sworn he heard a laugh—

'Are you all right?' Mum said, looking up from the television programme, a cartoon for infants. She seemed to have recovered from whatever had upset her before. 'Has something upset you? You're puffing as if you'd just run a marathon. Alex?'

'Nothing,' he said. 'I'm fine.'

Sarah cuddled into the crook of Mum's arm.

96

'I love this programme to death,' she said.

Stupid to frighten himself, he thought. At his age.

It had been a long dry summer holiday, the sun blazing every morning without fail when Alex woke at seven or earlier – the sun blazing all through the long day – the glow of the sun still clinging to the horizon when he went to bed at night.

'No holiday away this year, I'm afraid,' Mum said. 'We can't afford it.' Not many trips out, either. No money for the entrance fees or even the petrol. The car sat unused on the drive except for a weekly visit to out of town superstores and, twice, a journey down the motorway to visit Gran – Mum's mum. Since. Dad had left, Mum had refused to have anything to do with Dad's parents although, once, Alex was sure he'd seen their car parked on the opposite side of the street down the road. Alex had said nothing to Mum but he hadn't gone to speak to them either, even though both car doors had opened as he'd hurried his bike in through the gate. He hadn't looked back.

Occasionally, out of the blue, for Alex did his best to forget him, Sarah said, 'Mum, where's Dad?'

'Gone away.'

'But where?' Sarah would insist.

'To London. Barnet,' she added reluctantly as if Sarah was likely to jump up and go there that very moment.

97

'When's he coming back?'

'I don't think he will,' Mum would say gently.

'Never!' Alex said if Sarah asked him. How could Mum even pretend to be nice about him after all the terrible things that had gone on? He didn't have nightmares about what had happened, but sometimes during the day he'd find himself re-running events in his head like a video he couldn't switch off or look away from.

'It's the kind of weather people would pay thousands for if they were on holiday,' Mum said one particularly hot morning. 'Sarah's going to get sunstroke if she stays out in it much longer.'

In her swimming costume, the five-year-old was playing tea parties on that corner of the lawn – in fact she rarely played anything different, or anywhere else at the moment. And Alex had noticed Mum didn't like her playing there, for what reason he couldn't fathom, though occasionally he found himself glancing in that direction too – something about the spot, something about the obsessive way Sarah played her game. He wasn't sure what. Maybe something to do with that little laugh he thought he'd heard in the bushes – though scary things like that didn't happen in daylight.

'I'm going to sit outside,' he said.

'You're getting lonely. It's ages since your friends have been round,' Mum said.

'They're all away on holiday.'

'They can't all be!'

Perhaps they weren't but Alex didn't like leaving the house. When he did he felt as if he was deserting Mum. He hurried back as quickly as he could. And friends had ways of asking uncomfortable questions he wasn't ready to answer yet.

He made for the french windows.

'Don't hang around for my sake.'

'I'm not.'

He settled down in the deck chair in the shade of the house. Sarah was playing dentists this morning, although all the tea things had been set out.

'You've eaten too many sweets, you naughty person!' she was lecturing an imaginary patient. 'Now I shall have to do four fillings and pull three teeth out!'

'Don't hurt me! Please!' the patient pleaded in apparent terror.

'Come on! Open up that mouth! I've other people waiting. I'm very busy this morning indeed!' Sarah said sharply. 'Come on, now – I haven't time for this!'

'But I always brush my teeth after meals! *And* I eat lots of apples!' her other voice said.

Alex opened his book and found his place.

Ten pages later Sarah's conversation made him lose concentration.

'Two's enough! I don't want more!' she was saying.

'It would be lots more fun with more of us!' the other voice said.

A third, deeper, voice joined in. 'Yes!' it said. Alex looked up. 'We've told the others how much we enjoy ourselves and how nice you are. Just say yes and we'll fetch them.'

'Oh, I don't know,' Sarah said doubtfully. 'I really don't.'

'Go on!' her other voice said. 'Don't be a spoilsport!'

'Spoilsport!' the third voice echoed.

Alex closed his book. His sister was kneeling, facing his direction.

'But—!' Sarah said as if she couldn't make up her mind.

'Go on!' a voice said. To Alex the voice seemed to come from between him and Sarah.

'Sarah! Who are you talking to?' he said.

'What?' The five-year-old focused on him. 'I'm playing, that's all!' She turned away. 'Come on, everyone,' she said. 'Time to tidy up. I'm hungry.'

'I didn't know you were good at voices.'

'You don't know everything about me, do you?'

'Of course not!' a voice said close to his head.

Alex scrambled to his feet. Despite the boiling day there was an icy line of sweat across the back of his neck.

'How did you do that?'

'Do what?' Sarah gave him her 'you-stupid-boy' look.

'That voice.'

'That voice!' the voice said close to his ear, as if it was mocking him.

'Sarah!' It was Mum at the french windows. 'Time to eat. *Sarah!*' There was what sounded to Alex like panic in her voice. She came down the steps. 'How many times do I have to tell you?' Then suddenly all the things Sarah was playing with flew apart, a storm of temper. Teapot, toaster, cups, saucers, fruit flew in the air, came back to earth again and settled across the lawn.

Sarah was beside herself. 'Now you've done it! They'll never play with me again! They'll never come back! Never!'

'They?' Alex said. 'Who's they?'

'It doesn't matter! We'll pick everything up!' Mum said. She began hurriedly gathering things together. It seemed to Alex she was avoiding his eye.

'They?' Alex said insistently. 'Who's *they*?'

Neither Mum nor Sarah answered him but in the bushes two voices laughed.

'Hear them?' Alex shouted.

'Alex,' Mum said. 'Help, will you! Don't make things worse!'

★ ★ ★

'Voices. I'm not sure I know what you're talking about,' Mum said when Alex caught her on her own after they'd eaten.

'Yes, you do!' Alex challenged her. 'How long have you known about them?'

Mum ducked her head away. 'Sarah will be OK,' she said. 'Things will get better. We're all upset at the moment. It's difficult to adjust.'

'I'm not talking about Sarah. You know I'm not. They're horrible, they're evil!' Alex said. 'We've got to do something about it!'

'Go out and see your friends,' Mum said. 'Stop worrying. I know you're missing your father, but really what's happened has all been for the best. One day when you grow up you'll know that.'

'*I don't miss him!*' Alex shouted. 'I don't!' For a moment he was on the verge of stamping like Sarah in one of her tempers. Then he controlled himself. 'I really don't miss him, Mum. Honestly, I don't.'

Next morning, the weather had changed: no sun, low dark clouds, rain in the air. By the time they'd finished breakfast, it was pouring. Sarah didn't even bother to ask if she could go out. She settled in front of the television. About mid-morning there was a phone call. From Mum's tone of voice and the way she kept her voice down Alex knew it was from the solicitor who was handling his parents' separation and divorce.

Sarah couldn't possibly know who she was talking to but she said, 'When are we going to see Dad, Alex?' as Alex edged past Mum into the room.

He didn't answer.

'I want to see him.'

'He's never going to see us! They won't let him see us!' Alex said. 'Don't you understand anything?'

Sarah set up a wail. 'But I want to! I want to!'

Mum interrupted her phone call. 'What's the matter?' she called.

'Nothing.'

'It doesn't sound like it!'

'It's OK, honestly.'

Then, before Alex could stop her, Sarah was pulling the bolt at the bottom of the french windows. She yanked at the handle. A second later she was skidding across the patio and down the steps. The door swung and creaked. A rush of wet air came into the house.

'Sarah! Come here! You'll get soaked!' he called, low-voiced.

'What's happening now?' Mum called. 'I'm trying to have a conversation.'

But it was OK. For some reason Sarah had changed her mind. She stopped in the middle of the lawn, then turned and quite calmly began to walk back to the house.

'You'll be soaked. Mum will be furious,' Alex hissed at her as she came through the door.

'I don't care!' Sarah said.

'What did you think you were doing out there?'

'What do you think?'

Alex pulled the door to and leant down to do the bolt.

'Television!' an excited little voice said behind him.

'Better than parties,' another voice said.

'Lots of us now!' a third voice said.

'Yes! Lots and lots of us!' said another.

Alex felt a prod in the small of his back.

'Inside, now!' a voice said.

As the weather turned better again and the beginning of September loomed and the prospect of school, Alex began to get used to them. Whatever they were.

What were they after all? Just voices. Though could they just be that? There'd been that time they'd prodded him. Another time he was sure he'd been given a malicious pinch when he'd gone into Sarah's room. And when Sarah was in a temper, things would fly through the air and sometimes smash. Which was all right as long as she wasn't playing with proper cups and saucers.

They, and Sarah, seemed to be obsessed with playing houses and families. 'Can't you play anything else?' Mum would say irritably as Sarah set up yet another tea party. 'It's about time you had someone your own age to play with.'

The little girl or boy Mum dragged round never lasted long. Usually their visit ended in tears.

'Why are you so beastly to them?' Mum said in desperation. She was looking tired, seemed almost to be growing old in front of Alex's eyes. 'It was the last straw, him refusing to sell the house,' he heard her say to Gran on the phone one night. 'I want to move, to get out of here. Sometimes I hate this place. I want to get rid of it.' Then one morning they all went down the doctor's and Alex and Sarah sat in the waiting room under the eye of the receptionist while Mum talked to the doctor for ages. After, she went to the chemist's for pills. At least she became calmer, even if she didn't seem any happier.

At least they didn't bother him. When he was lying in bed at night he heard their voices in Sarah's room next door while her black and white portable played into the early hours. Mum said nothing. She seemed to have given up on Sarah. There were phone calls from the school complaining about her behaviour, asking if she wasn't sleeping. Mum went down the first time; after that she did nothing. 'Voices?' Sarah said the one time Alex tried to talk to her. 'You do say funny things, Alex.'

'The children?' he heard Mum say to Gran another night on the phone. She lowered her voice. 'Sarah's rather naughty at the moment, but it'll pass. But Alex—' He didn't hear the rest except for something about 'bottling it up'.

★   ★   ★

'Remember Maisie?' The neighbours were talking in the next-door garden. It was the weekend, early September, good weather. Alex was on his own on the lawn, Sarah playing upstairs in her bedroom.

'Maisie who?' Mr Thomas mumbled, half-asleep.

'Maisie Stuart. Who else?'

'Maisie from next door? What about her?'

'I bumped into her the other day down at Tesco's.'

'I thought they'd left the district. How is she? Still as batty as ever?'

'A different person,' Mrs Thomas said. 'She's got over her troubles. Right as rain she seemed. Didn't look a day older than when they left – what was it? – six or seven years ago?'

Then a lorry went past, grinding its gears. 'Voices!' Alex could have sworn Mr Thomas said; something about voices. Alex lost the rest of the sentence. When the noise of the lorry had died away they were talking about someone else.

Above him, through Sarah's open bedroom window, the voices drifted.

October. The nights drawing in. Leaves across the lawn and pavements. Frost one morning on the hedges and verges as Alex made his way to school.

The voices were still there, but there didn't seem to be anything you could do about them. Sarah denied their existence. Mum ignored them. Sarah spent almost all her time in her room now, rarely putting in an appearance downstairs, and Mum let her. Mum was more cheerful but in a remote sort of way, not bothering too much about meals on time or whether they wiped their feet when they came into the house. Even Alex could see the house was getting dirtier by the day. Sarah's room in particular was a tip, toys and clothes strewn everywhere. It was as if Mum had abandoned it.

Then one evening when Alex arrived home from school there was a change. The house had been spring-cleaned from top to bottom. Surfaces sparkled with polish. The lounge had been tidied. In the kitchen everything was back in place. The windows had been cleaned.

'What happened?' he couldn't help saying.

'I'm going out tonight,' Mum said. 'Someone's invited me. We're going to the cinema, then for a meal. I'll be back by half eleven. Heather and Jane are coming to look after you.'

'From across the road?'

'That's right.'

Heather and Jane were the baby-sitters from the old days when Mum and Dad had used to go out together.

'Who are you going out with? Do I know them?'

'His name's Daniel. You've never met him. You needn't worry—'

'I'm not.'

Sarah hated the idea, though. First there was a flood of tears. And then the paddy. Her bedroom door slammed so hard you heard its frame vibrating.

'You shouldn't let her get away with it, Mum!'

'She still thinks her dad wants to come back.'

Alex's heart missed a beat. 'He doesn't, does he?'

'I wouldn't let him if he did.'

'That's all right, then. Doesn't he ever say he wants to see us?'

'The solicitor's never said so. I'd tell you—'

Alex wondered. 'Mum—' For some reason it was the first time he felt it worthwhile asking her about the conversation he'd overheard through the hedge. 'The woman who lived here before us – she heard voices, too. Mr Thomas said—'

'Mr Thomas is an old gossip,' Mum said. 'Talk about women gossiping!' She moved away towards the kitchen. 'I'm going to cook your and Sarah's tea, something special tonight, Alex,' she said. 'Cheer up.'

Alex didn't see the man when he came to fetch Mum – only his back as they went down the front garden path. The tree by the gate half-hid his car which seemed large and shiny and new.

Heather was eighteen, Jane a couple of years younger. 'About time your mum got out a bit,' Heather, who was tall and rather thin, said. Her sister who was shorter and almost as skinny said, 'What's up with your Sarah?'

'She's sulking. You can guess what about.'

'Understandable,' Heather said, 'though I don't mean it as a criticism of your mother. She's got her own life to lead, hasn't she?'

Jane went up to try and persuade Sarah down. She came back a couple of minutes later.

'She won't open her door.'

'My go next!' Heather said. Alex followed her to the bottom of the stairs to listen. Sarah said nothing as Heather talked to her through the door, but the voices were in an absolute frenzy. Alex waited for things to be thrown but as Jane joined him, Sarah's bedroom door opened.

'More luck than me!' Jane said. 'But then Heather can always twist people round her little finger.'

'Didn't you hear them?' Alex said as they settled down on the settee.

'Hear what?' Heather said.

'The voices.'

'What voices?' Heather looked at him curiously. 'Hearing things now, are you? You'd better watch it, young man!'

Later, nearer twelve than half past eleven by the clock on his bedside table, Alex heard the car park outside the house, hurrying footsteps on the path, Mum's apologies in the hall, Jane saying, 'It just doesn't matter. Honest.'

After Jane and Heather had gone and the clink of tea cups had finished in the kitchen the man's voice remained. Then Sarah's door opened. He heard his sister pad across the landing and edge step by step down the stairs. He heard Mum's surprised, 'Sarah! What are you doing up?' and the man's deeper voice greeting her.

Later, much later, when the car had gone, Mum brought Sarah back up. She was ages in her room settling her off. Then the crack of light round Alex's door widened and Mum stood looking down at him. He kept his eyes closed.

'A pity you weren't awake. You could have come down too,' Mum said softly. 'Sarah got on with him ever so well. You would have done, too. I think Sarah will be happier now. Not, of course, that I'm saying anything about me and Daniel. We've only gone out once.'

You didn't invite me, Alex thought. *You left me upstairs.*

'Well, goodnight,' Mum said. Alex felt her lean over him. She put a kiss on his forehead. She closed the door and went downstairs.

There was silence for a minute then the voices said, 'She didn't invite you. She didn't invite you, did she? You must hate him, that man. You want your own dad, don't you?'

'This is a comfortable room, isn't it?' a lone voice observed.

'Yes, better than hers,' others answered. 'I don't know why we stayed there so long.'

'We'll be comfortable here, won't we?' the lone voice said. It sounded so like Alex's own. 'We'll stay for ever!'

'Yes! Yes! Yes!' the voices said. 'We'll stay for ever!'

THE WILD PLACE
by Diana Hendry

It began with a dare. Tommy Roebuck stood on an upturned dustbin and pointed his finger at me.

'Titch Farrell,' he said, 'I dare you to walk through the Wild Place at night.'

'I dare you, too!' I yelled, hoping he'd back down. I must have been mad! Tommy Roebuck, the roughest, toughest boy in our school, back down on a dare? Never!

'You're on!' he said, jumping off the dustbin that had somehow survived the full weight of Roebuck might and muscle, *plus* Doc Martens. 'Shake on it!'

When Tommy shakes your hand it's a wonder you've any bones left in it afterwards. Tommy swaggered off – he lives at the top of my road – and me and my squashed hand went home.

Actually all of me felt pretty squashed, quashed, squiffed and crushed and it wasn't just the thought of the Wild Place, at night *and* with Tommy Roebuck. Nor was it the thought of how, in the murky, spooky dusk, the sand-hills of the Wild Place loom up at you, all pale and ghostly like the hills of a strange planet. No, all that was bad enough, but what really scared me was that I knew what Tommy's dare meant. It meant he had singled me out to be his best mate.

Don't get me wrong. He was no bully, Tommy Roebuck. It was more what my sister, Jess, said – 'That Tommy Roebuck likes a little kid as his mate so he can look even bigger and tougher.'

And that's how it was really. Half the small kids in our year had been best mates with Tommy Roebuck. He wore them out (like people wear out shoes) with his dares and adventures. Steve Miller, Tommy's last best mate, had ended up in the Royal Infirmary with a broken leg. A skateboarding dare, that one. And the funny thing was that although Tommy was forever coming up with dares, no-one *dared* say no to him! What would he do if anyone said 'no'? No-one had found out, but I guess we all feared that it would be more than a hand that got squashed to a pulp.

Well, that was the state of play. Tommy and I were to walk through the Wild Place soon after dark the next night. The dare was on. We'd pledged, sworn and shaken on it. It was un-get-outable. So when we heard about the Wodwo, the creature who haunted the Wild Place, it was too late.

We heard about the Wodwo the very next morning. The day of the dare itself.

It was our teacher, Miss Triggs, who told us. We'd been doing this project at school, you see, looking at Meols as it used to be in the old days. Miss Triggs had brought a book in with pictures of Meols when it was just a fishing village. (We liked the old lifeboat best and the way it was pulled down to the sea by horses, and manned by men with funny nicknames like 'Four Eyes Jones' or 'Long Ted Beck'.)

But that day Miss Triggs had a different story to tell. 'Once upon a time,' she said, 'all of this place was just a wilderness. It was known as the wild land of Wirral. Beneath our sand-hills there lies a buried forest.'

It gave me goose pimples when she said that – or maybe I should say ghost pimples – thinking of all that wildness buried under the ground and waiting to get out. Aching to get out, I thought, because you see, apart from the Wild Place, our village was so *tidy*! All the houses in straight lines and the trees lined up to match. Even the sea was tucked in tidy behind railings – like a prisoner behind bars. Sometimes the tidiness of our village made me hanker for a bit of wildness, something to match the untidiness – maybe even the wildness – inside me.

Tommy and I exchanged looks and I knew we were both thinking the same thing. A wilderness. The Wild Place.

To my surprise, I suddenly found myself feeling a bit better about the dare. Scared, yes. But excited, too. Those sand-hills that I'd never thought much about were actually centuries old. We'd be travellers in time, Tommy and I.

'There's a very old story,' said Miss Triggs, opening a book, 'about a knight called Sir Gawain. One winter he journeyed through this wilderness as a dare. There were ogres panting after him and he had to fight dragons and wolves, bears and boars. When he came to the forest there were huge grey oaks, a great tangle of trees all covered in shaggy moss. That's where the Wodwos lived, and Gawain had to fight them too.'

Miss Triggs turned to the book. ' "Had he not been a strong fighter and stubborn, and had not God preserved him, beyond doubt he would many times have been slain and left there dead",' she read.

'Please, Miss, what's a Wodwo?' asked Tommy, sticking his big hand up.

You could tell Miss Triggs was pleased to have Tommy's attention for once. 'A sort of troll or wild man of the woods,' she said, smiling brightly at him.

Tommy looked over at me and smirked. It was his 'nothing-scares-me' sort of smirk.

'I bet that Wodwo is still there,' he said on

the way home. 'I bet he's still haunting the Wild Place.'

'Don't be daft,' I said, though I'd got the ghost pimples again. 'That was all a long time ago. That old forest is buried and the Wodwo is buried with it.'

'Wodwos don't die,' said Tommy. (You could tell he was really enjoying himself now.) 'They stay alive for ever, moaning and trolling and looking for the lost forest. You'll see. You'll see tonight!' And off he went, moaning and trolling up the street.

'How do you know?' I shouted after him.

'I can feel it in my bones!' Tommy shouted back.

Now if you ask me, there's far too much flesh covering Tommy's bones for him to feel anything inside them. But as for me, if bones could chatter like teeth, that's how mine felt, soon after tea when I met Tommy at the agreed place on the street corner. That moment of excitement when I'd thought of us, Tommy and me, as travellers in time had vanished. The only place I wanted to travel to right then and there was my bed with a nice cosy duvet tucked round me.

It didn't help that we'd both had to fib. The Wild Place was strictly out of bounds at night. I'd said I was going to Tommy's to check on some homework. He'd said he was coming to my place. Actually, I'd half hoped my mother would stop me going out, but all she did was raise an eyebrow and say, 'So

Tommy Roebuck does homework these days, does he?' And I'd pretended not to hear so I didn't have to answer.

Funnily enough, Tommy didn't look quite so big and swaggery now. Perhaps it was just the dusk light making the houses seem taller. And perhaps it was the streetlights that made him look pale.

He was wearing his black anorak, and when I punched him in what I hoped was a good, tough-guy kind of 'hello', my fist met armour-plating.

'Books!' said Tommy. 'Against the claws of the Wodwo.'

The way he said it, I wasn't quite sure if it was a joke or not. I tried a bit of a laugh, but Tommy didn't join in so I changed it to a cough.

I suppose Miss Triggs might have been pleased to think that Tommy had *some* use for books. I wished I'd thought to do the same. My own once fatly-padded anorak had worn thin and flat in the wash. The claws of a friendly tabby cat could have ripped it off me. Did Wodwos have claws? I began to wish that Miss Triggs had told us just exactly what that old knight, Gawain, had done to fight them off and, more importantly, if he'd killed them all, or . . . had he left one or two?

I think Tommy was wondering something similar because he'd started to walk really slowly, scuffing his feet in his Doc Martens so that for one brightly hopeful moment I thought, 'Does he want to call off the dare?' And then I cancelled the thought. Tommy Roebuck, call off a dare? Never!

When we reached the Wild Place the sand-hills seemed to have grown in the dusk. Their shapes were like enormous cornets of grey ice cream melting into darkness. It was like walking into an awful dream. A nightmare. And it was spooky the way our footsteps vanished in the sand as if *we* were ghosts, as if we were like Gawain, journeying through the wilderness, eyes alert for panting ogres, dragons and wolves, bears, boars . . . and yes, Wodwos. Wodwos with claws.

The deep dunes between the hills were the worst. We reached them after about twenty minutes. By then our boots were so heavy with sand we had to take them off and hang them round our necks, tied by the laces. Down in the dunes you couldn't see Meols at all. It had vanished from sight as if Tommy and I had dropped down, down, down into another world. The Wild-Land-of-Wirral world.

Then the moon came out and the hills made large shadows as we crept between them, and the sand shifted and glinted under it as if any minute something . . . someone . . . was going to rise up out of the wild ogre-ridden past.

It was terribly, horribly silent. A sort of padded silence that made you think that if you called for help no-one would hear you. Sometimes the sand would slide down behind us with a soft little slithering hiss

such as a creeping Wodwo might make. And once a distant squeal of car brakes made me jump.

'It's really weird here, isn't it?' I whispered, because I didn't quite dare break that awful silence. But Tommy just said, 'Shut up!' in a voice that wasn't quite his usual voice. But then nothing was very usual that night.

It didn't help that Tommy kept looking over his shoulder and when a seagull flew over with a wild, shrieking 'kee-owk! kee-owk!' he covered his head with his hands as if he thought that Wodwos not only had claws, but were like bats that could fly down and snatch you.

'Have they gone? Have they gone?' he asked.

'It was only seagulls,' I said.

'Course it was,' said Tommy in that same funny voice. 'I just can't stand seagulls.'

It came back to me then how Tommy had said, 'Wodwos don't die. They stay alive for ever, moaning and trolling.' And somehow it was as if he'd come to believe his own story.

And now I'll tell you something really strange. As we walked down in the depths of the dunes, like the ghosts of ourselves, I realized that Tommy was shivering. And not with the cold, because it wasn't cold. The dunes were like the thick walls of a house keeping out the cold and the wind. No, Tommy Roebuck, big Rough-Tough-Tommy (as he was called), Tommy who would dare anyone anything was shivering with FRIGHT!

Then all of a sudden he flung himself flat in the sand.

'Wodwos!' he hissed. 'I can see them!'

I flung myself down beside him. Then I realized what he'd seen. The moonlight had thrown our shadows – shadows twice as big as us – up the side of the dunes. Our anoraks gave us funny shapes. What Tommy had seen was the silhouettes of two enormous creatures stalking us like two wild trolls in some desert horror film.

'It's only our shadows,' I said.

But Tommy had his head buried in his arms and wouldn't look.

And just as suddenly as Tommy had flung himself in the sand, I realized what was really scaring him. I had this flash as if someone had switched on a torch in my head. There was nothing in the *real* world that scared Tommy Roebuck. Dare him to climb the tallest tree, walk the narrowest wall, dive off the highest diving board, skateboard down a one-in-six hill and he'd do it. No problem. I bet a gang of burglars wouldn't scare Tommy Roebuck.

What *did* scare him was the *un*real world inside his own head. The imaginary ogres lurking there – and in particular, the Wodwo. I reckon that Wodwo had grown in Tommy's imagination ever since Miss Triggs had 'planted' him there that morning. After all, it had grown claws by tea-time, hadn't it? It had become fierce enough in Tommy's mind to make him pad his anorak with books. It had grown bat's wings.

It was my moment of triumph. All I had to do was get up, dust the sand off myself and say, 'OK, Tommy. Dare over. I'm going home,' and leave him there, shivering in the sand, not daring to look up. And I thought of doing it. I really did. Only when I'd persuaded him to lift his head just enough to look at me, I saw he was crying. Sand and tears all in a gritty mixture on his face. It's bad enough seeing a small kid cry. But a big kid, like Tommy – well, it was awful.

'Look,' I said, 'I've brought my torch.' (Maybe it had been the torch hidden in my pocket that had magicked a flash of torchlight in my head.) Until that moment I hadn't planned to tell Tommy about either kind of torch. He'd only have sneered at me for being scared of the dark. Now I beamed the real torch up and down the sand-dunes. 'Whatever you saw has gone,' I said, 'and if we climb up that dune we'll be in sight of Meols again.'

Tommy sat up then. 'Sand in my eyes,' he said, wiping his face with the sleeve of his anorak.

'Doesn't half sting,' I said, pretending I had some too.

Then we began scrabbling up the dune together. And that was the best moment really, because all at once I knew I wasn't scared. More than that. I knew

123

I *liked* the wildness of the Wild Place. I liked the feeling that it was haunted, that once upon a time there'd been a forest here with bears and wolves and yes, even Wodwos. Somehow all the history of the Wild Place, the thought that there'd been people here before me and before me and before me – including some ancient old knight, clopping along on his gee-gee and probably just as scared as Tommy – made it, well, homely!

I thought, too, that if the ghost of old Gawain could see us now, Tommy and me, he'd probably give us some kind of medieval salute. Some sort of 'hail fellows, well met' – a greeting sent across the desert sand of centuries to those who dare. Sir Gawain and I, Rough-Tough Titch Farrell, were journeying together through the Wilderness of Wirral. After this I wouldn't care about being scared my bike brakes would fail going down the big hill, or sometimes still wanting the landing light on at night.

I was thinking all this as we skidded on our bums down the other side of the dune. And then we saw it. A small, black, flapping figure hurrying – hungrily? – towards us. All I saw before I clutched Tommy and Tommy clutched me, was one enormous Eye glaring at us. Our boots hanging on our chests bumped as loudly as our hearts.

'It's moaning!' whispered Tommy.

'Has it got claws?' I whispered back, because suddenly I didn't feel a bit like Sir Gawain any more and because I was so scared I'd closed my eyes.

'I daren't look!' Tommy answered and we both froze there, hanging on to each other so tight that we both jumped when a voice – a very familiar voice – said, 'Tommy Roebuck! Titch Farrell! I'd know you two anywhere!'

And there was our black-clad troll, our very own Miss Triggs, looking quite amazingly ordinary in her long winter coat and with not a claw in sight. She was carrying a bicycle lamp – the Eye.

'Playing Wodwos, are you?' she asked rather crisply, tilting the lamp to look at us. 'And I suppose your parents know you are here?'

'Well, not exactly, Miss,' I said. 'Not exactly playing Wodwos and they don't exactly know – our parents, I mean, Miss.'

'Perhaps a little *exact* homework would be a good idea,' said Miss Triggs in that extra sweet voice she uses when she knows she's caught you out.

'Shall we say that for *exactly* the next week you will both be on time and your homework will be on time and that maybe . . . maybe we won't need to mention this little episode to anyone's parents?'

'Yes, Miss,' we both said together.

'Well, then,' said Miss Triggs, sounding as plump with satisfaction as a Wodwo might sound after a good meal of boys. 'Let's all go home. I've been to see my mother,' she continued, quite chatty now, the way teachers are when they've got their own way, 'and I often walk home this way. I like thinking of the wilderness that used to be here. And the forest. You can feel it, can't you? A sort of haunted feeling.'

Tommy, shoving his feet in his boots, said nothing.

'It's all right,' I said, casual as I could.

Miss Triggs pulled her coat about her. 'Well, I'm glad it's only you two I met,' she said, 'and nothing scarier.' I could have sworn she was smiling.

Tommy and I attempted a polite kind of laugh, though I have to say Tommy's sounded more like a grunt.

'See you tomorrow,' said Miss Triggs. 'With home-work!'

'Of all the people to meet!' I said when we were back in our street, back in the real world of tidy houses, street lamps and trees.

'Better her than a Wodwo!' said Tommy. Then he grinned at me. 'You know something,' he said, 'I was dead scared in there, in the Wild Place.'

And then I swallowed hard because Tommy Roe-buck had done it again. He seemed to grow before my eyes and become big, tough Tommy once more, brave enough to admit he'd been scared. And after what seemed a very long time and in a voice that came out more like a squeak, I said, 'Me too!'

Tommy's still my best mate. In fact we've been best mates for six months now. Perhaps it's just because I've shot up a bit recently, and no-one calls me Titch any more. They call me by my proper name, Greg. But I don't think that's the only reason.

It's more that now that I know that everyone – even a big kid like Tommy – is scared of something; somehow that makes me feel . . . well, less scared of everything.

I think Tommy must feel a bit like that too because he's given up dares these days, and because Miss Triggs gave him his first ever 'A' for his story, 'The Night I Met a Wodwo'.

JON FOR SHORT
by Malorie Blackman

*Muffled footsteps sounded in the darkened bedroom. Dim
torchlight danced eerily across the walls. The footsteps slowed
as they approached the bed. Carefully, silently, the torch
was placed on the bedside table. A brilliant flash of metal
glinted in the torchlight. The glare of a knife blade . . .
And as the blade flashed downwards, it seemed in the dim
light to be winking, winking, winking . . .*

'Of course not! To tell the truth, I feel kind of
sorry for him. It would've been better for him if he'd
died . . .'

At first I thought I was still dreaming, but then I
realized that the voice was outside my head – for
once – not inside. So I had to be awake. I turned
my head in the direction of the woman's voice and

opened my eyes. The nurse jumped back and stared at me. She'd obviously thought I was fast asleep. She was ancient – fifty-something at least – with greying hair, swept back into such a severe ponytail that it pulled her eyelids out towards her ears.

'I just came in to make sure you were all right.' The nurse's voice was steady, but her lips were a thin slash across her face. 'Can I get you anything?'

I shook my head. She left the room without a backward glance. I closed my eyes wearily and was instantly asleep again. My nightmare washed me away like a tidal wave.

A brilliant flash of metal glinted in the torchlight. The glare of a knife blade . . . And as the blade flashed downwards, it seemed in the dim light to be winking, winking, winking . . . Arms came up to ward off the flashes of light, but it did no good. The flashes just grew harder and faster. Harder and Faster . . . HARDER AND FASTER . . .

When I woke up this morning, my left arm had been taken. I knew it was no longer there because it hurt so much. My left shoulder roared with pain. I'd only experienced pain like it once before – when they took my right arm. That was just under (just over?) a day ago. (A week ago?) In this place, I've lost all track of time. But this place is all I have.

Because I can't remember . . .

What's wrong with me? Why did they take both

my arms? I don't know. My mind's an empty box. I want to remember. I really do. I get the feeling the doctors don't believe me when I say that, but it's the truth. It's just that, every time I try to force myself to remember what happened, what brought me here, the memory dances away from me like a shadow in a darkened room. Every morning I wake up and the memories are *almost* there. But when my mind reaches out for them, they slip away, more elusive than water in a sieve.

My name is Jonathan, Jon for short and I'm . . . I'm eleven, almost twelve. Just remembering that much leaves me exhausted. I turn my head from left to right, looking around. I'm in hospital. I've been in hospital for a long time – only I can't remember why . . . I can't remember seeing this room before either. Have I been moved? If so, from where?

It is a small room, with light-coloured walls and a door to my left, but apart from the bed I lie on (I assume it's a bed), there is nothing else in the room. The only light comes in through the small, frosted pane in the door.

The door to my room slid open. I waited a few moments before turning my head. In spite of the pain, I had to be careful. I couldn't show anyone just how terrified I was. And how lonely. I looked at the nurse who stood by the door. His eyes were stone cold, stone hard. He didn't like me. That was very obvious. *But why?*

'I'm Nurse Jennings,' the man said, looking away.

I wanted to ask about my arms, but my voice refused to work. And the nurse still refused to look at me.

'I've come to give you your medication,' Nurse Jennings continued. 'I'm going to roll you over onto your side so that I can give you an injection in your bottom. Doctor Jacobs will be coming to see you soon. She's a psychiatrist. Just a moment.'

Nurse Jennings disappeared out of the room, only to return moments later with the elderly nurse who'd checked on me during the night.

'Joe Forman, number J42935,' the elderly nurse said.

'Joe Forman, J42935,' Nurse Jennings repeated.

I shook my head. That wasn't right. My name was Jon, not Joe. They'd got the wrong name.

The elderly nurse scooted out of the room without another word. Nurse Jennings rolled me over and jabbed me in my bum. It should've hurt, but it didn't. I couldn't feel a thing. Nurse Jennings turned me onto my back. I smiled at him. I wanted so much for him and all the other nurses to like me. Being so alone was hell.

'Keep smiling,' Nurse Jennings said, straightening up. 'It won't do you any good. You won't pull the

wool over Doctor Jacobs' eyes. And I'll tell you something else . . .'

'Thank you, Nurse Jennings. That will be all.'

'Oh, Doctor Jacobs, I was . . . I was just . . .' Nurse Jennings trailed off.

I gave up trying to smile. It didn't feel right. Nurse Jennings left the room. Doctor Jacobs slid the door shut and walked over to me. My head began to feel fuzzy, muffled, like it was being stuffed with cotton wool. And heavy. So very heavy.

'That's it, Joe. You go to sleep. It's the best thing for you.' Doctor Jacobs' voice came from long ago and far away.

It's Jon, not Joe. I wanted to tell her that, but I couldn't open my mouth. I fought against falling asleep. I *couldn't* fall asleep. That was when the nightmares came . . . But it was no good. I couldn't keep my eyes open. Moments later, I was washed away again.

HARDER AND FASTER . . . His legs kicked off the bed covers, kicked up towards the glinting and winking. The flashes of light moved up and down, up and down – striking at his arms, his legs. He twisted and writhed . . .

I opened my eyes slowly. The room was dim with evening light. And then the pain started. My knees were on fire. I knew what that meant. They'd taken more of me. My legs below my knees were gone. I bit down onto my bottom lip until my mouth filled with blood. My whole body shook with pain and dread. Whimpering noises burst through my lips which were still clamped shut. I couldn't help it. Scalding tears burned my eyes. If only the pain would stop. If only . . . The door to my room slid open. Doctor Jacobs entered.

'Good! You're awake,' she smiled. Then she saw the tears on my face.

'D–Doctor Jacobs, please, *please* give me back my legs,' I pleaded. 'I didn't say anything when my arms were taken but you shouldn't have cut off my legs as well. I didn't deserve that.'

Doctor Jacobs frowned deeply. 'There's nothing wrong with your arms or your legs. Look for yourself. You still have limbs. We haven't done anything to them.'

'PLEASE . . . I WANT THEM BACK,' I shouted at her. 'You all skirt around me and whisper about me. You want to drive me crazy. But I won't let you do it. Do you hear? You're the ones who are crazy. You just wait till my mum comes to see me. You just wait . . .'

'Joe . . .'

A nurse ran into the room.

'Get me 50 mgs of Pethidine,' Doctor Jacobs commanded.

The nurse dashed out again.

'Now then, Joseph . . .' Doctor Jacobs began.

'Stop calling me that. My name is Jonathan.

135

JONATHAN. I know what you're doing. You drug me until I'm senseless and then you cut off my limbs one by one . . .' Tears streamed from my eyes. Phlegm ran from my nose. And I couldn't wipe it away. The pain in my knees was easing slightly now, but what did that matter? I'd lost more of myself. I'd cried in private for my arms. But to take my legs as well . . .

Doctor Jacobs walked over to me and threw back the bed covers.

'Look! There are your arms, your legs . . .'

I glanced down, in spite of the fact that I knew she was lying. My legs below my knees and both my arms weren't there — just as I knew they wouldn't be.

The nurse came back, carrying a small tray. Doctor Jacobs picked up the hypodermic needle from the tray and immediately injected it into the top of my thigh. Within seconds, my head was fuzzy again. The doctor handed over the needle to the nurse. She left the room at once. The doctor laid a cool hand on one of my thighs.

'Joe, can't you feel that?' she asked. Her frown was so deep that the creases around her mouth ran down to her chin.

'My thighs are still there,' I sniffed, impatient with this game the doctor was playing. 'It's the rest of me I'm talking about.'

I swallowed hard. Come on, Jonathan, control

yourself, I thought sternly. Don't let them drive you crazy. Don't let them . . .

Doctor Jacobs just shook her head slowly.

'Can I have some water, please?' I whispered.

The doctor picked up the plastic tumbler beside the bed, filled it and held it out to me. I just looked at her. She pulled a tissue out of the box on my bedside table and wiped my eyes and nose. Pursing her lips, she then bent over me and placed the tumbler to my mouth. I drank thirstily. I would have drunk the whole glass of water but Doctor Jacobs removed the tumbler before I'd finished. I licked my lips slowly. My tears slowed. The pain in my knees was reduced to a dull throb.

'Doctor Jacobs, please don't let them take any more of me,' I begged softly. 'Please . . .'

She regarded me, shaking her head again. I wondered what the strange expression on her face meant. It was a mixture of pity and something else which I couldn't quite make out. There was a knock at the door.

'Joe, you have to go for an X-ray now. I'll see you when you get back,' Doctor Jacobs said.

'I'm not going anywhere,' I said, turning away. A porter I'd never seen before lifted me up against my will and put me in a wheelchair. As he wheeled the chair along the hospital corridors, he spoke to me.

'Why did you do it?'

'Do what?' I asked slowly.

'Do what? Are you serious? You . . . Y-You . . .' The porter spluttered and coughed as his words tripped over themselves in an effort to come out. Then he clamped his mouth shut when he realized how ridiculous he sounded. I too kept quiet. I hadn't been trying to provoke or goad him. I genuinely didn't know. *I couldn't remember.* As he pushed me along, I struggled to keep my eyes open as the painkiller took over. I failed . . .

The flashes of light moved up and down, up and down – striking at his arms, his legs. He twisted and writhed . . . His legs kicked out, kicked hard – but it didn't do any good . . .

When I awoke, I was back in my bed – and the rest of my legs had been taken.

My whole body was numb. I lay perfectly still, staring up at the ceiling until Nurse Holmes walked into my room, a dinner tray in her hand. Nurse Holmes didn't like me. But then, no-one really liked me. It'd always been that way. If I could only remember why . . .

'I suppose there's no point in asking you to feed yourself.' Nurse Holmes' lips curled downwards with contempt.

I didn't bother to answer. We both knew I had no chance of feeding myself. My arms had been taken. Why did she have to be so cruel? Nurse Holmes sat down on the bed beside me.

'What is it?' I asked, turning my head slightly to look at the tray in her hands.

'Mushroom soup and a lamb casserole.'

I didn't like meat but I was starving. And I had to eat. I had to rebuild my strength. The sooner I was strong again, the sooner Mum could take me home. I'd be back with Mum – and my brother, Joseph . . . *I had a brother called Joseph*. At last, I'd remembered something else about myself. And that explained why they kept getting my name wrong. They were confusing me with my brother. I closed my eyes, trying to conjure up his face. Disappointed, I couldn't remember anything about him. Was he older or younger? Did I have any other brothers or sisters? Lots of questions. No answers.

Nurse Holmes took the plastic cover off the soup and removed the plate-warmer from the casserole. She stood up and turned to me.

'You might have some people fooled with this act of yours, but I'm not one of them,' she hissed. 'You can feed yourself or starve.'

And with that she flounced out of the room. I lay there, smelling the lamb and the soup. I had no legs to push myself up with. No arms to feed myself. I was so hungry, the smell made me feel sick. I closed my eyes and willed myself not to mind about the hunger so much. I had to think of some-thing else. To take my mind off my stomach, I concentrated on my heartbeat. It beat more slowly than before they'd taken away my limbs.

What did I look like?

No . . . I didn't want to see myself as I was now. I knew I wouldn't be able to bear it.

Think of something else, Jon, I told myself.

Although I concentrated on the slow beat of my heart, the rumble of my stomach was louder. I decided to go to sleep. To sleep for as long as possible. After all, what else was there for me to do? What else could they take? And maybe this time, the nightmare wouldn't come.

His legs kicked out, kicked hard – but it didn't do any good . . . He turned towards the light. And I saw his face for the first time. Only it wasn't his face. It was my face. His body – my face . . .

'Joe? Joe, can you hear me?'

I opened my eyes slowly. It was Doctor Jacobs. She sat on the bed and smiled and asked me all kinds of questions. I gave her what answers I could but all the time I was trying to drive my nightmare out of my head. It wouldn't budge.

Doctor Jacobs asked, 'Joe, do you remember what happened two weeks ago? Do you remember the reason you were brought to this hospital?'

I shook my head. 'My name is Jonathan, Jon for short. And no, I don't remember. Why won't anyone tell me?'

'Do you really want to know?' the doctor asked softly.

'Yes, I do. I want to know why everyone here hates me so much. I want to know why you've stolen my legs and my arms. I want to know . . .'

There was a long pause.

This was it. Now I would find out why I was here. I had to know. I needed to remember.

'I'm going to take a chance, here,' Doctor Jacobs said at last. 'I think you should know what happened – what you did. I think you're ready. And it will help you.'

And very slowly, very carefully, she told me. 'Joe, you had a brother called Jonathan. He was your identical twin brother. You weren't close. In fact, according to your mum, that's an understatement . . .'

And she carried on. I heard her words but they bounced off me until there were too many of them to bounce off and they sunk into my flesh like razor-sharp barbs – and still she spoke. My body shook with horror and the more I shook, the more my body hurt.

And still Doctor Jacobs spoke. I wanted to yell, to howl and not stop. It was all lies. It had to be lies. I would never, could never, do that – the mindless, horrific thing she spoke of. I wouldn't do that to anyone, let alone to my own twin brother . . .

'No . . .' I whispered. 'No, it's not true.'

I had to do something to drown out her words. My shoulders started to hurt. My hips started to hurt. I covered my ears with my hands and sat up, drawing up my legs.

'NO! NO! NO!' I battered at the doctor with my fists. 'LIAR . . . LIAR . . .'

All at once the room filled with people. I was pushed back onto the bed. I battered at them all. Battered at them with my fists and kicked at them with my feet until the room swallowed me up like a whirlpool. Doctor Jacobs and the others faded to nothing. There was just me and my brother left in the whole, wide world. Jon lay there, looking up at me, his eyes burning into mine. His blood drenched the bed sheets. It dripped down from the knife in my hand – dripdripdrip . . . He whispered my name over and over before he died. Joe . . . Joe . . .

When I awoke this morning, they'd taken my whole body. There's nothing left of me now except my head and my brain, sitting in the centre of this pillow. I don't know how they're keeping me alive – I don't care. I just wish someone would tell me what I did to deserve this. I really *do* want to know. What did I do?

I wish . . . how I wish I could remember. All I know for certain is that my name is Jonathan, Jon for short. And I'm eleven, almost twelve.

UNCLE MATTHEW

by Jan Mark

Lucy, sit down for a moment, I need to talk to you. If your friend's waiting he can wait a bit longer. In any case, I don't see any friends out there, unless—

Look, Lucy, when I was your age – don't kick the skirting board like that. Sit down. This isn't going to be a lecture, it's a story, and I meant what I said. I was exactly your age.

It was two days after my birthday and I went into town to buy some new football boots. Dad – your grandpa – had given me the money for them as a birthday present. He'd promised me the boots but Mum – Granny – said, 'You'd better wait till September before you buy them, the rate your feet are growing.' She was just thinking of games lessons at school, but my dad knew that I needed them that

143

minute. We played football all year round, of course we did. Outside of school there was no cricket season for us.

It was June so there were no sales on – no, there *weren't*, not in those days. Sales happened in January and July. Anyway, the sports shop had none I could afford so I went over to Debenhams, where they had a big shoe department.

Lucy, I know you're not interested in football, but just listen.

It was like our Debenhams, not quite so big, but like a maze inside. You had to work your way through the perfume department and ladies' hosiery, handbags – you know how it is, and it was all bright lights with mirrors everywhere; little ones on the make-up counters, tall tilted ones among the shoe racks, big oblong ones on the pillars that held up the ceiling. Everywhere I looked I could see myself coming or going, sometimes three or four of me, from the side, from the back, all heading in different directions. And I noticed something that I didn't usually see – when one mirror reflected another, I saw myself as I really was, not back to front, like when you look directly at yourself in the glass.

The first time, I couldn't think what was strange about it, then I started to experiment. I shut my left eye and the face in the mirror shut its left eye. Usually when you do that, the mirror image shuts its right eye.

I forgot all about the boots. I just wandered around, tracking myself from mirror to mirror, making faces, waving my hands. I'm surprised the store detective didn't follow me in case I went completely mad and started smashing things. Maybe he did – I never saw him.

But what I did see, in a little mirror on the glove counter, was me looking over my own shoulder, and then the second face slid out of sight, which wouldn't have bothered me except that I hadn't moved.

I turned round. A little way off, between two racks of coats, was a glass that showed me full-length. I'd wandered into the menswear section by that time. It was darker there and they didn't have so many mirrors. Well, I stood and looked at myself and then I raised my right arm and saluted. The boy in the mirror raised *his* right arm and saluted back. That shook me because I was standing dead in front of this mirror, only two or three metres away from it, so it had to be reflecting *me*, not reflecting a reflection of me. So I took a step forward, and the reflection took a step back. I went cold then; something was wrong, something was terribly wrong. I couldn't move. But the reflection moved, it shrugged its shoulders, turned and walked away, sort of nodding at me to follow. It was limping. I wasn't limping, and I saw that where the reflection had been, there was no mirror at all, just a big white sign with black letters saying VISIT

145

OUR NEW COFFEE SHOP ON THE SECOND FLOOR.

I didn't want to visit anything; all I wanted to do was get out, but I was too shaken to move. I wasn't frightened yet, but I was shivering, standing there alone between the two rows of coats, all those shoulders level with my eyes, like standing between two ranks of soldiers and nothing in front of me but that notice: VISIT OUR NEW COFFEE SHOP ON THE SECOND FLOOR.

Then all the shoulders on the right started heaving. Someone on the other side of the row was riffling through the hangers, and somebody pushed behind me and I unfroze. I turned round then and went back out, not running, sort of floating through all the mirrors, watching myself coming and going in my blue jeans and white T-shirt. And as I went, I realized what had seemed so wrong before. The person who had confronted me between those coat racks, he had had my face, but he hadn't worn my clothes.

He'd been wearing short trousers, fairly short, just above the knee – yes, I know shorts come down to the knee these days, but they didn't in 1969. Shorts were short, and no-one wore them in the street, no-one my age. And he'd worn a grey shirt and a grey knitted pullover and long grey socks. And a tie, a sort of school tie, with stripes. If he hadn't looked like me, he'd have looked like William – you know,

146

William Brown and the Outlaws, in the books. But he didn't have a cap on.

I went home. Mum said, 'Didn't you get the boots, then?' and I said, no, I'd decided to do what she'd said and wait till September.

My voice sounded strange. She looked at me hard and said, 'You've been out in the sun too long. You're as white as a sheet.'

I tried to be funny. 'I ought to be brown if I've been out in the sun too long, oughtn't I?' But I've never been brown. People with hair the colour of mine don't tan; we stay pale or we burn. That boy I'd seen in Debenhams, he'd had my hair; my hair and my face.

I've never believed stories about people who meet their doubles, because most of the time you'd never recognize your double. What you see in the mirror isn't what other people see. By now, I didn't know *what* I'd seen, *who* I'd seen, and when Mum sent me to lie down I went into the bedroom and hung a sweater over the mirror so that I wouldn't have to see it again.

I couldn't go on avoiding mirrors for ever, the house was full of them: one on the wall of the bathroom, Dad's shaving mirror with the magnifying glass that made you look like the creature from 20,000 fathoms, two in the hall, one over the mantelpiece in the front room, a little one in the kitchen and two or three in my parents' room. Very gradually I brought myself to start looking in them, but the only face that looked back was mine. It raised its right eyebrow when I raised my left. I suppose I was hoping to discover that it was all a trick of the light, but I wasn't really fooling myself. What I'd seen in the menswear section hadn't been in a mirror at all.

Mum kept me in for a couple of days and then the weather broke. We had a thunderstorm and it got cooler. One evening I went down to the rec on my bike with my old boots slung around my neck. I just fancied a good kick-about in the mud. All my mates were there and we belted up and down for about an hour. It started to rain again, but we didn't care. It felt like the real thing, after the heatwave; mud and rain and a soggy wet football.

As I said, all my mates were there, and one other. I didn't notice him at first, we were all pounding up and down, skidding about, falling over. Although it was almost mid-summer, the clouds were so heavy that the air was dark and thick, more like an autumn evening. The rain came down harder, and in the end we packed up and wandered off in twos and threes. I sat down on a bench to change back into my shoes, and when I looked up I saw someone standing on the path that led between the rec and the allotments. It ran from Church Lane to the main road, and on one side there was a chain-link fence that was all trodden down where we took short cuts into the rec.

In his grey shirt and sweater and shorts, and his

long grey socks, he was the same colour as the twilight. He wasn't transparent, but I couldn't see which side of the fence he was standing. And that's all he did. When I raised my right hand to wave, he just stood. We weren't playing games now.

I called out to him, 'What do you want?' because that's what I felt, that he wanted something.

He didn't answer, but he looked me full in the face, as he'd done before. And now we were away from all those mirrors he looked more like me than ever, but not exactly like me. He was thinner and taller, but otherwise pale and freckled . . . with that red hair. Only his was cut short and clippered up the back. I wore mine long like footballers did – like everyone did then.

I yelled at him, 'Why don't you leave me alone?' but he just smiled, as he'd done before, in Debenhams, and turned his back.

I'd told him to leave me alone, but I didn't like it when he started walking away. I jumped over the fence where it was squashed flat, and went after him; left the boots and the bike and chased him down the footpath. He didn't seem to be running – he was still limping – but I couldn't catch up. He was always ahead of me and I saw nothing else, just that grey figure in the rain. I saw nothing else when we got down to the main road, I didn't even see the road, till someone shouted and grabbed me by the shoulder, just as I was running across the pavement, just as I was about to run straight under a lorry. I saw these great wheels go by, as tall as I was, and a frightened, yelling woman who'd dropped all her parcels in a puddle to drag me to safety.

'What were you doing? What did you think you were doing?' she kept saying, and shaking me. She was crying with fright. In the end I sort of came round and said something about some big boys chasing me.

But I was the one who'd been doing the chasing, and the person I'd chased was standing on the other side of the road, watching us. I knew she hadn't seen *him*.

I don't remember going back to the rec, but I must have done, because when I got home I was wheeling my bike with the boots dangling from the crossbar.

Mum was out, round at a friend's, when I got in, but Dad was there. They'd never have left me to come home to an empty house, thank God.

He sent me off to get changed – it was raining stair rods by then and I was soaked. When I came down again he'd made me some drinking chocolate and he said, 'As I understand it, that's the second time in a week you've come home looking like death warmed up. What's the matter?'

How could I tell him? I didn't know *what* to tell him, but I knew he was keeping an eye on me, after that.

I was keeping an eye on me, too, in the mirror,

in all the mirrors. But the next time I saw my grey friend it was out of doors again, on the cradle bridge over the railway. That was what we called it, a footbridge made of iron girders, high up over a cutting where the line came out of some woodland.

I usually cycled to school, but I'd got a puncture, so I took the short cut over the bridge that day. I was walking on my own, and as I came towards the bridge it seemed to be empty, but as soon as I set foot on it I saw him, at the far end, just climbing up onto the girders. He gripped the handrail, swung his leg over behind, as if he was getting on a bike, and then seemed to be on the other side of the girders, and vanished.

I kept walking towards the end of the bridge. The sun was shining where I was, I remember my shadow beside me on the wooden boards, but his end was shaded by trees. When I reached the place where he had been sitting I looked over, and there he was on the side of the cutting, down below. He saw me watching and waved, beckoning.

But this time he had given me too much warning, he had moved too soon, for when the express from Dover came thundering round the curve, he was dancing on the rails in front of it. But I was still at the top of the cutting. I don't recall doing it, but I had climbed up the girders and over the side of the bridge.

I didn't go to school. If I'd thought that I should

find my mother at home, I'd have hidden in the woods all day, but she was at work. It was my father I wanted to talk to, and I knew where to find him. He worked shifts, and when he was on nights he went straight from the factory to put in an hour or two on our allotment, the one next to the rec.

I had something to ask him that I couldn't bring myself to ask Mum.

As I stumbled along the grass paths I could see him by the little shed he had built from old railway sleepers, drinking tea from his thermos and smoking a cigarette.

He might have said, 'Why aren't you at school?' but he had more sense than that. He just looked at me and said, 'Hm, three frights in a row. *Now* will you let on?' He poured some more tea and gave me the cup.

I said, 'Dad, tell me, please, was I ever a twin?' For that was what I'd been wondering, what I'd been sure of, that I must have been born with a brother, a brother who had died before I could know him and had now come back to haunt me, a brother my age who looked just like me.

Dad lit another cigarette, then he said, 'No, you were never a twin. But I was.'

Now, Lucy, you've got all your grandparents, two of each, but I had only my mother's mum for a gran and Dad didn't have anyone by the time I came along.

'I was the younger one, Mark,' my dad said. 'Matthew was seventeen minutes older. We were inseparable, went everywhere together, did everything together; except once. We came through the war without a scratch, even though we lived in South London, but a year before it ended, 1944, I went to a party without him. He'd sprained his foot and couldn't walk much. I wanted to stay home with him, but he said, "No, you go. One of the sisters is engaged to a Yank. You might get some chewing gum."

'When I came home, the house had gone. Half the street had gone. A flying bomb had cut out overhead. We all lost someone. I lost my parents, my grandparents, and my brother Matthew, my twin.'

He was put in a home, he said. And then he told me that for the rest of that year he kept seeing Matthew, at the home, at school, in the street, limping ahead of him, and always Matthew was smiling, waving, beckoning him to follow. And at first he did follow, but then he began to notice that the places Matthew beckoned him towards were not very safe places; scrap yards, railway lines, busy roads. In the end, after he'd nearly broken his neck falling down a cellar on a bomb site where Matthew had led him, he decided that next time Matthew called him he would stay put. And he said that Matthew kept trying, but after this he started getting harder to see and in the end, after about a year, after their next birthday, Matthew disappeared altogether.

'And now he seems to be back,' Dad said to me. 'Well, he'd every reason to want me to join him, but he's got no call to fetch *you* away. What's he tried so far?'

So I told him about the lorry, and the cradle bridge. 'But he's not like you, Dad,' I said. 'Even his hair's different.'

'Oh, no,' my dad said, 'we weren't identical twins. You're not much like me, either, but you're just like him.'

And as he said it, I looked up, and saw Matthew, my uncle, a little way off in an old greenhouse. There was mainly just the frame left but I knew it was full of broken glass, like razors.

And for about a year afterwards, just as my dad had done, I saw Matthew here and there, always smiling, always beckoning, always limping, wearing his shorts and his shirt, his pullover and his long grey socks. I never followed him again.

You've seen him too, haven't you? Oh, Lucy, don't deny it. You've never been one for dangerous games; no climbing trees or walking on walls for you; not even rough sports. You're happiest with your Sindy dolls and little ponies.

But Lucy, I saw you on your birthday, fooling on the rails by the mill dam. I saw you yesterday on your bike, on the slip road to the motorway.

Where were you going today with your friend, your friend who is waiting, the friend I cannot see? I haven't seen him for twenty-six years, since he was eleven, since I was eleven, since I was your age. I told you, didn't I; exactly your age.

Oh, darling, don't follow him, do as I did, do as my father did. Smile and walk away. He wants you to join him, as he wanted us, but don't do it, don't do it.

We'll all join him eventually. He will just have to wait.

THE AIRMAN'S SIXPENCE
by Helen Dunmore

She keeps me up with her every night. It's as if she doesn't want to be alone. Even though it's nearly eleven o'clock now, she's just put three more big logs onto the fire. My cocoa steams on the wonky tin tray. She keeps back enough milk for my cocoa every night, and even sugar. Two spoonfuls. She always saves her sugar ration for me. There are biscuits as well. She watches me eating and her face is hungry. It's no good trying to hide a biscuit for Billy. She sees every move I make.

'Drink up, dear. Don't you like your cocoa?'

'Mmm, yeah. Course I do,' and I pick up the thick white mug.

'There's no need to say "yeah", Ruby. After all, we aren't Americans.'

'No, Mrs Penbury.'

'Auntie Pauline, dear! You silly girl.' And she laughs, a tinkly laugh that's a bit frightening because it doesn't seem to belong to her. Mrs Penbury is big, and she's as strong as any man. She does a man's job. She's always telling us that. Men have to be hard.

The wind whines round the farmhouse. It sounds as if it's fingering the walls, trying to get in to us. But I don't mind the wind. I strain my ears for what I think I can hear under it. Yes, there it is. A sound that's even thinner, even sadder than the wind. I glance quickly at her, and clatter my mug down on the tray to cover the sound. Has she heard? She's frowning, staring at her feet. What if she gets up, goes to the stairs, listens? What if she hears him? I'm sure it's Billy. He'll have had another of his bad dreams.

Billy's five. He never used to have bad dreams, till we came here. We were in London before, with Mum, then before that we were down in Devon, with Mrs Sands. She was lovely. But she couldn't take us back when the bombing started again, because her daughter, Elsie, had a new baby. Mum didn't want to send us away again, but she got a job in the factory at nights, and that meant she couldn't take us to the air-raid shelter if a raid started. I would've taken Billy. I'm old enough. But Mum wouldn't let me.

'*No, Rube. With you and Billy safe in the country, at least I've got peace of mind. I know I'm doing right by you.*'

It was all right in Devon with Mrs Sands. We missed Mum, of course we did. But not like this. Not with a pain that gets worse every morning when I wake up and know we've got another day here.

It *is* Billy. I know it is. He's crying again. He isn't properly awake yet, or he wouldn't make a sound. He's crying in his sleep. I shuffle my feet, crunch my biscuit, slurp the rest of my cocoa.

'I'm ever so tired, Auntie Pauline. I think I'd better get to bed.'

She stares at me. 'I've only just put those logs on the fire,' she says, 'Don't you want to sit up a bit longer?'

She always wants me to sit up. I don't think she wants to be on her own. She likes me to keep talking, it doesn't matter what I say. When it's quiet, she looks as if she's listening out for things I can't hear.

But I've got to get to Billy. I stand up, and put down my mug. I'm supposed to kiss her goodnight now. I've got to do it. She mustn't know that I don't like kissing her, or she'll be worse than ever to Billy. Her hair bristles against my face.

'G'night, Auntie Pauline.'

'Goodnight, Ruby. There's a good girl.'

There's a little oil lamp for me to carry up and undress by. Billy has to go up in the dark. She pretends it's because he's too young to remember about the blackout, and he might show a light. Billy is frightened of the dark. I go up the creaky stairs with my lamp flame shivering and bobbing on the walls. They are rough, uneven walls, because this is an old house, right on the edge of the village and well away from the other houses. It's a lonely house. Maybe that's why she wants me to sit up with her, even though at home Mum would've sent me to bed ages ago.

The whimpering sound is getting louder. I hurry. She mustn't hear it. I know what to do. I've got to wake him up really gently. I kneel down by his bed and put my arms softly round him. He's sitting up but I can tell he's still asleep. His eyes have that funny nightmare look in them. He is cold. I cuddle him close and whisper, 'Billy, it's all right. It's only me. It's Ruby.'

I keep on cuddling and whispering. Slowly his stiff body relaxes. I can feel him coming out of the dream and waking up. I press his face into my shoulder to hide the noise.

'It's OK, Billy, Ruby's here.'

He's shaking. Perhaps he's ill? But I look at his face by the oil lamp and I see he's crying. Fear pounces on me.

'Oh, Billy. You haven't. You haven't gone and done it again.'

And he nods his head, crying and shivering.

'Never mind. Don't cry. Ruby's here.' I hold him tight, tight. He's only five. My little brother, Billy.

'*You look after Billy, Rube. You know how he gets his asthma.*'

That's what Mum said when she was waving us off on the train, the second time we were evacuated. She thought it would be like Mrs Sands' again, and so did we. Billy was all excited, jumping up to look out of the window, waving at Mum. '*You look after Billy.*' Yes, I was right. He's wet himself. It's not his fault. It happens when he's asleep. He can't help it. But she mustn't find out. What can I do?

I can't do anything. She'll find out. She always does. And she'll put Billy in the cupboard under the stairs again, for hours and hours. It's dark in there. She says it's to teach him. '*He can't go on like this, Ruby. What'll your mum say when she gets him back, wetting the bed every night? She'll think I don't know what's right. Sometimes you've got to be cruel to be kind.*' He doesn't cry or scream when he's in the cupboard. I think she thinks he doesn't care. Oh, Billy. '*He's a boy, Ruby. No good bringing him up soft. You won't be doing him any favours.*'

Suddenly I make up my mind.

'Stand still, Billy, while I get your clothes. We're going home.'

I scrabble through the drawers. Clean pants, clean trousers, Billy's warmest jersey. His winter coat is on the hook downstairs. I'll get him dressed then we'll both get into bed and wait, wait . . . Once she's gone to bed, we'll go. We'll go home. Mum wouldn't want us to stay here. I know she wouldn't. She'll be working now, she works nights in the factory, but by the time we get to London it'll be morning. I don't care about the bombs.

When the last sound of Auntie Pauline going to bed has died away, we wait to give her time to go to sleep. I've blown out the lamp and it's dark. But I know my way round the house, even in the dark. I know all its lonely corners.

'Billy. Ssh. Hold my hand.'

The stairs don't creak. The kitchen door opens and there's the smell of the slack she's put on the fire to bank it up for the night. Billy presses up behind me while I slide the big bolt back, very very slowly. It squeaks like a mouse. She hates mice. She's always leaving poison for them. The yard door swings open and black cold night air fills the space in the door-frame.

'Wait there, Billy. Don't move.'

I sweep my hand along the dresser. There it is. Her fat black purse with the big clasp. I weigh the heavy purse in my hand. My mum always said she could leave a penny out on the kitchen table all week.

'*Ruby'd never touch it. Would you, Rube?*'

'*No, Mum!*'

I was so proud of that. Mum let me go to her purse and get the shopping money out, because she knew

I'd never take a penny off her. Now I unsnap Auntie Pauline's big purse and feel inside. Two heavy half-crowns. A couple of joeys. A sixpence and a florin. I take them all and wrap my handkerchief round them. Is it enough to get us to London?

I hold Billy's hand tight as we shut the kitchen door behind us. The yard is full of shadows and we dodge through them to the gate. The lane is a tunnel of night.

'We can't go through the village,' I whisper to Billy. 'All the dogs'll bark at us. We'll go down the lane and across the fields.'

My chest hurts. Billy's too little, he can't run like I can. I hoist him up and carry him but he's too heavy for me and I can't carry him for long. He runs a bit, then I carry him, then he runs again. Each time I pick him up, he's heavier.

'You're a good runner, Billy!' I tell him, to keep him going.

The wind rustles the trees over our heads. There are sudden shapes and shadows. Something barks. Maybe a fox. We know about country things now. Then we come round the corner of the lane and a bit of moon shines on a big puddle. The road forks three ways.

'I got to put you down, Billy.'

He flops up against me. It's his asthma. Mum never ever lets him go out at night.

'All right, Billy, we'll have a rest.'

There's a stile and a path going across the fields. But no signposts. They've taken them all down in case the Germans come. Just the three lanes pointing off into the dark, and the path across the fields. Nowhere to say where the railway station is.

'You better now, Billy?'

He looks up and nods. I know he isn't, really. I stare round, trying to guess, trying to remember which direction the station is. We came from the station, off the London train. But it all looks different in the dark, strange and different.

'You wait here a minute while I look down the lane.'

But he grips me tight. 'Don't leave me, Rube!'

That's when I see it. A little red light that grows strong in the dark under the trees, then fades. Then it brightens again. I know at once what it is. My mum smokes and sometimes she comes in and sits on my bed in the dark and I watch the red tip of her cigarette winking at me. Someone's smoking, there under the trees. Someone I can't see. I grab hold of Billy. As we stare, a big shadow peels away from the trees and moves into the lane. It's a man. A man smoking. A man in uniform.

I know all the uniforms. I peer through the dark and I see the shape of him. RAF. Straight away I feel a bit better. I like the RAF. He'll be on his way back to camp. Probably been to a dance. He throws away the cigarette and it skitters down the air and

dies on the wet road. Then he walks slowly towards us as if he's been waiting for us, as if he knew we were going to come.

'Hello.'

I don't answer. But Billy pipes back, 'Hello' to him.

'You're out late,' said the airman. He's got a village voice, not a London voice like us. He must be from round here. I wonder where?

'Yeah,' I say. I look at him hard. Is it OK to ask him? I can see him quite well now because the clouds have blown back from the moon. But there's the shadow of his cap, too, hiding him. I clench my hand in my pocket, and it knocks against the money I've stolen. She'll be after me. She'll get me. They'll all believe her. *A thief. A little thief.* No-one'll believe I had to do it because of Billy, except Mum. I've got to get to Mum.

'We've got to catch a train,' I say. 'My mum's ill.'

'Oh,' he says. 'The London train? The milk train?'

'Yeah. The milk train.'

Then I think, *How did he know it was London I wanted?* But I don't ask.

'It's this way,' he says, pointing across the fields. 'It's only a mile, across the fields.' Then he says, 'I'll go with you. Make sure you get there safe.'

Everything my mum's told me about strangers floods into my head.

'It's all right,' I say quickly. 'We can find it.'

'Over this field. Turn left at the stile and follow the hedge. Then there's a gate. Straight over and across that field and you come to the road. Turn right and it takes you all the way.'

'Is there a bull?' asks Billy in his growly voice. He thinks every field's got a bull in it.

'Couple of cows if you're lucky. Turn left, keep going, cross the gate, keep going, turn right at the road. You got that?'

'Yeah.'

'Mind you look after Billy.'

Did he say that or was it my mum's voice in my head? No, he did. *How did he know Billy's name?*

'You got money for the train?'

My hand closes over *her* hard, cold coins.

'I got money.'

He looks at me. 'You took it, didn't you? You don't want to go taking her money.' He digs his hand in his pocket and brings out a handful of notes and coins. He picks out two pound notes and a ten-shilling note and holds them out to me. But I step back.

'It's all right,' he says, 'You take it. I've no use for it now.'

So I do. I feel as if I've got to do what he says. Then he gives Billy a sixpence. 'Buy some sweets with it,' he says. Billy looks down at the sixpence and up at the airman. He doesn't smile or say thank you. Billy's always quiet when he's pleased. The man

167

puts his hand on Billy's head, and rumples his hair as if he knows him.

'Give me that money of hers,' he says to me. 'I'll put it back for you. Then you're all straight.' I like the way he says it, as if he knows how I'm always all straight at home, with Mum. I'm not really a thief. I give him the handkerchief, and he unknots it and takes out the money. He puts it away carefully, in a separate pocket from his own money, then he looks at us again. This time the moon is full on his face. He is sort of smiling, but not quite, and under it he looks sad. He reminds me of someone. He looks like someone.

'Don't hold it against her,' he says. 'She can't help herself.'

I say nothing. He sounds as if he knows Auntie Pauline better than I ever could.

'Go on, then,' he says. I climb the stile, then he swings Billy up and over. I take Billy's hands and jump him down. 'I'll stand here,' says the airman, 'just to make sure you take the right turning.'

When we get to the other side of the field we look back and he's still there. He waves, pointing left, and I wave back to show I know what he means. Then we climb up the next stile, and over, and the hedge hides him. We go as fast as we can. There's no time to talk, but once we're safely on the road, Billy pants out in his growly whisper, 'He's still watching us.'

'How d'you know?'

'He just is.'

The wind blows round us, cold and sweet and smelling of cows and country things. We stop to catch our breath and listen. Ahead of us there's the shunting noise of a train and I know we're nearly there.

'Don't worry, you're not going back,' says Mum. She's been working all night. She's worn out and here we are on the doorstep and what's she going to do with us? But it doesn't matter. Nothing matters now we're home. Billy's thinner and his chest sounds worse and when I tell Mum about the cupboard under the stairs she says she's going straight down the Evacuation Office to sort it out this very minute and we're not to move till she gets back. She goes off without even changing out of her overalls.

It's a long time before Mum comes back. Billy's asleep and I think I've been asleep, too. Things are all muddled up in my head. The airman, the dark lane, the feel of Auntie Pauline's money. How could he put it back? Mum flops into her chair and shuts her eyes.

'They're going to get on to her,' she says at last. 'Course, there's always another side to the story. Did she ever talk to you about her son, Ruby?'

'I didn't know she had a son. She didn't like boys.'

'He was in the Air Force. Died on a bombing raid last year. That's why she took you kids in, for the

169

company. It must have been hard for her. Sent her a bit peculiar, I dare say, all on her own out there in the middle of nowhere, grieving for him. Not that it's any excuse, mind.'

'*Don't be too hard on her. She can't help herself. Give me the money, I'll put it back.*'

Mum sighs. 'I could murder a cup of tea,' she says.

'I'll make it,' I say quickly. I want something to do.

'Good girl. Seems she was so proud of him, being in the RAF. Oh, this war's got a lot to answer for. I suppose it got to her, other people's kids being all right when hers had gone.'

'But she was all right to me.'

'You're a girl, Rube. You wouldn't've reminded her of her son.'

I remember what Auntie Pauline was always saying: '*No good bringing a boy up soft. You're not doing him any favours.*' Was she thinking of her boy, and the war that was waiting for him when he grew up? I put the match to the gas and wait for the kettle to boil. I listen to the water begin to hiss in the bottom of the kettle. It's a sleepy, peaceful sound, and I shut my eyes.

Moonlight shines on the airman's face. He looks like someone I know. Who is it? The answer itches at the back of my mind but I can't quite reach it. He smiles. Then I know. It's Billy. The airman looks like Billy. So that was it. Mum was right, it was because Billy reminded Auntie Pauline of her own son that she was so hard on him. But perhaps she didn't mean to be . . . perhaps she thought she was doing the right thing . . .

The kettle changes its note and starts to sing. I open my eyes and look at Billy, sleeping on the kitchen settle. His face has a bit of colour in it again. His hand is shut tight, even though he's asleep, and in it there's the airman's sixpence.

FANTASTIC SPACE STORIES
Collected by Tony Bradman

10, 9, 8, 7, 6, 5, 4, 3, 2, 1 . . . We have lift off!

In this fantastic new collection of space stories, you'll travel on board Starskimmer 1 the galaxy-flying starship, experience life in a Martian colony, be trapped inside the cavernous guts of a bubble – and undergo a serious sky-jacking in deepest, darkest outer space!

Blast off into other galaxies of aliens, patrol-droids, stun-guns and koptas, in these ten gripping stories by authors including Nicholas Fisk, Malorie Blackman, Helen Dunmore, Douglas Hill and Mary Hoffman. An anthology that's truly out of this world!

'A first-class collection' *The School Librarian*

Other collections compiled by Tony Bradman:

AMAZING ADVENTURE STORIES
A STACK OF STORY POEMS
GOOD SPORTS! A BAG OF SPORTS
  STORIES

0 552 52767 X

GRIPPING WAR STORIES
Collected by Tony Bradman

Tommy gripped the rifle in both hands and strained to listen as he crept through the Bosnian forest . . .

For Tommy war is only a game but for plenty of other young people it's a desperate fight for survival. Ahmed is sent to London as a refugee from sniper-scarred Sarajevo; Dafna is desperate for decent food when Jerusalem is besieged. Anton is caught up in a dangerous Resistance plot in occupied Amsterdam; and Younger Bear, a Cheyenne warrior, prepares for his first battle. The war zones are scattered across the globe but the excitement, the unpredictability and the terror of war touches them all.

Tony Bradman has collected ten inspiring stories of action, courage, fear and friendship in wartime which are sure to have you gripped to the very end.

0 552 54526 0

GOOD SPORTS!
A BAG OF SPORTS STORIES
Collected by *Tony Bradman*

Jump into this bag of sports stories and pull out hours of action-packed reading. Every one a winner!

Dive into the bag and meet . . . Dan, a talented swimmer who discovers an exhilarating new sport; Judith, who is determined to play in a tennis tournament; Sanjay and Michael, who run into trouble when they are picked to play for the school cricket team; and many other lively characters taking part in a variety of sports – from football and athletics to ice-skating, trampolining and skateboarding.

From a team of top children's authors including Robert Leeson, Michelle Magorian, Jean Ure, Jan Mark and Anthony Masters.

'A great read for sports-mad youngsters' *The Junior Bookshelf*

0 552 54296 2

SENSATIONAL CYBER STORIES
Collected by Tony Bradman

Boot up your imagination and log on to this sensational collection of cyber stories.

A bit of hacking for fun goes seriously wrong when a rogue computer program sends out the secret police to arrest the school boy hackers; a boy swaps his brain with his computer's memory, and amazes all his friends with his command of facts and figures; and virtual reality becomes blurred in a thrilling but dangerous game . . .

Ten incredible stories involving state-of-the-art technology and real human excitement from top children's authors including Malorie Blackman, Helen Dunmore and Paul Stewart. Guaranteed to tempt even the most addicted game-player away from the computer screen!

0 552 54525 2